ISLAND *of* ELANDRIAL

ALPHENA

authorHOUSE®

AuthorHouse™ UK
1663 Liberty Drive
Bloomington, IN 47403 USA
www.authorhouse.co.uk
Phone: 0800.197.4150

Published by AuthorHouse   04/08/2016

ISBN: 978-1-5049-9772-0 (sc)
ISBN: 978-1-5049-9771-3 (hc)
ISBN: 978-1-5049-9773-7 (e)

Print information available on the last page.

Any people depicted in stock imagery provided by Thinkstock are models,
and such images are being used for illustrative purposes only.
Certain stock imagery © Thinkstock.

This book is printed on acid-free paper.

Because of the dynamic nature of the Internet, any web addresses or links contained in
this book may have changed since publication and may no longer be valid. The views
expressed in this work are solely those of the author and do not necessarily reflect the
views of the publisher, and the publisher hereby disclaims any responsibility for them.

For my children,
who I love with all my heart;
Thank you for giving me the time to write this.
Thank you to others who have helped me along the way;
your ideas have made the story what it is.
This is my legacy to my children.

Elandrial
Beautiful views
Clearest of waters
Mythical creatures
My home

CHARACTERS

Caturn – land of the humans
Gladonis – king
Itisha – queen
Zaferia – princess
Glador – mage
Liza – servant to Zaferia
Ivan, Luka, and Rogue – sovereign guards

Falor – land of the humans and dragons
Drakus – king
Zeva – queen dragon
Marcus – mage
Theolis – sovereign guard

Atalonia – land of the wolves
Tristan – alpha-king
Damoc – second in command

Tolemaz – land of the pegasi
Konrad – king
Wade – mage
Alex, Chad, and Eric – guards

Drawde – land of the harpies (all female)
Abila – queen
Silvanus – mage

CHAPTER 1

"Zaferia, we cannot stay long." I turn to my friend and nod, taking my usual seat at the water's edge, admiring the way the water cascades over the rocks down to the pool below, fascinated with how clear the water is. Willows as old as time stand on either side of the waterfall with branches reaching the pool, covering the waterfall in almost a thin blanket of green, brown, and silver. The jewels sparkle when the sun hits them. I close my eyes, feeling the slight breeze swirling around, hearing the sound of the water hitting the rocks and the birds chirping happily away. I sigh as I open my eyes to look around, and I notice how all the different trees surround the waterfall, almost protective from a stranger's eyes, yet the grass reaches the forest walls and almost comes to my waist. Letting my imagination run wild, I imagine a small castle over by the trees, the brightest of flowers here, a high tower in the middle of the castle so that I can look over the waterfall. I have always wondered what was beyond.

Gasping, I realise that there are goose bumps all over my body. He is watching me again. A feeling that I cannot explain travels all through my body. I glance over my shoulder, and there he is, the bluest of eyes staring back at me. You could lose yourself in them if you were not careful. I try to look away, but he is like a magnet. There is simply one word to describe him: "magnificent". His body looks as if it would feel like the finest of silks, and his hair is the shiniest of chestnut locks hanging down to his shoulders. Sighing, I manage to turn away to look at the waterfall. The goose bumps disappear, and I know he has gone. I wish I knew who he was, his name, anything.

This beautiful man appears in my dreams every night and has done so for the past two years. Only this last week has he appeared in the shadows.

****

Drakus watches the princess. Her hair, the softest of browns, hangs past her slender shoulders, blowing in the breeze. He sighs, knowing he cannot step forward. When she turns, he swears his heart has stopped beating. He has to force himself to stay in the shadows, for the guards will strike otherwise, but oh, she is breathtaking. He forces himself to return to Zeva, his loyal dragon.

****

Liza, my servant and friend, tells me it is time to return home. Reluctantly I leave the waterfall carrying another beautiful quartz crystal for my collection. They remind me of the man who haunts my dreams. With the guards behind us, the walk back to the castle is a short one through the forest, and I find it peaceful here; always have. The forest feels so alive and free with the suns shining through the trees, hitting the ground. I notice flowers are growing. I'm tempted to pick a few, but I don't. There are plenty of flowers in the courtyard to pick as long as the gardener does not catch me. Last time he said I cut the roses wrong; I didn't realise there was a right way. The last thing I picked were daisies for a crown and necklace. Admittedly that was last week; they are hanging over a stone on my mantel in my room.

"My lady, if I may," says Liza, breaking out of her thoughts.

"Yes Liza, you may. Please call me Zaferia." I look at Liza when I say this.

"You seem troubled, my lady; what is wrong?"

"Liza, do you ever have a feeling that all that we have in life is a test to challenge us if we are capable?"

Liza looks at me as if debating the question. "My lady. That is a difficult question to answer, as we come from different places and every person's challenges are different. It is figuring out the right path to take that is the challenge."

Walking through the long grass, I think about this all the way to the palace with the grass tickling my fingers. I walk through the courtyard where the ivy has grown higher, almost reaching the top of the wall, and I notice the gardener from the corner of my eye. I see him tending to the rose bushes; he is picking some for the castle vases. They are the colour of rubies; the smell in the castle will be amazing. I hope he picks some different-coloured roses this time, as he only ever picks red ones though there are roses of every colour you could imagine.

Upon reaching the castle, I notice the new gates that are tall, pointy, and as gold as the king's crown. Liza takes the correct position behind me; this always irritates me, as Liza is more of a friend than my servant. I hold my head high as a princess should do. I go to my room, passing all of the servants and guards with nods of greeting. Once at my room, I place my beautiful quartz crystal in the dish with the rest and lie on my bed while Liza runs me a bath. Our castle is a fine one, made of the strongest stone; and with the towers being round, there is a great view over the lands. Candles have been placed up the stairs to the top; I think this is romantic, though my father thinks it is just light for the bowmen. Who am I to argue with the king and his decisions?

I don't think my father ever realised Rogue and I used to steal the serving dishes from the kitchen and slid down the stairs many a time. Oh, the fun we had till he joined the sovereign guards; then he became a bore. The castle is nearly as old as the land itself, and the ivy grows up half of the castle and has surrounded the west side of the castle completely. Fighting for light through the windows becomes a battle every now and then. My room is in the middle of the castle, and I insist on having a candle on every step. I think they bring out the colours in the family portraits that are on the walls. I agreed to have no candles near my ancestors' tapestry of dragons and wolves fighting; the colours are so vivid and spectacular. Walking along the corridor to my room, I look out of the tiny windows. I was once obsessed with the idea that a monster could fit through there. I must have been very small, as I can only get my arm out of there now; but looking out I can see the horses grazing in the pastures, and beyond that is the forest, which by the way is massive. If you go to the roof, for as far as you can see we have land around the castle with lots of different animals: chickens, goats, sheep, geese, ducks, pigeons, and pigs. Beyond this there is my waterfall.

Somewhere beyond the trees is Byrond, the local town that sells all of the finest foods and trinkets which I buy for my mantel. Well, something has to match the quartz crystals. Looking at my bed I realise the wood is a deep cherry colour and the thin, sheer-looking material rests against every post on my bed. I want to rip it down. What a waste of material; it should be over my window or could be used to block my door.

I walk over to my mantel and stroke the quartz as though it is my dream man's face. I move towards all my trinket boxes; some were given as gifts, and some I managed to buy. "Liza, we need wood for the fire; it is almost out, Liza."

Liza pokes her head around the bedroom door from the bathroom "My lady, which herbs do you require for your bath? May I suggest lavender to calm your mind?"

"Lavender sounds heavenly." I smile at her sweetly.

"Very good, my lady."

She knows me all too well.

Once the bath is drawn, I dismiss Liza. I stay in the bath, thinking of the man in my dreams, staring into his eyes as though he is standing in the room with me. When I realise my teeth are chattering, I get out of the bath and wrap my robe around me. Walking back into my room, I smile; Liza has placed my night clothes on the bed and fresh logs on the fire. Climbing into bed, I can see the moon through my window; it's full, and the skies are clear. I fall asleep dreaming of the man who watches me from afar.

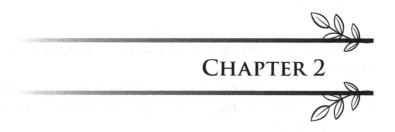

CHAPTER 2

I wake in the morning to the birds singing and the sun brightening up my room. I think of my dream man and why he stays in the shadows at the waterfall. Do I dare approach him?

Liza comes in to prepare me for the day ahead. "My lady, you are due for breakfast with the king and queen." Reluctantly I get out of bed and have a wash, and Liza helps me dress.

I walk to the breakfast room and greet the king and queen; then I take my place at the table. Mother and Father always sit at opposite ends of the table. It is a long table; they must have to shout to each other and look around the hundreds of flowers and candlesticks placed on it. I sit in the middle so I don't have to shout. For breakfast we have the usual: eggs, bacon, sausage, and a fresh roll, which I eat quickly.

"Mother, Father, good morning."

"Good morning, my little princess." I roll my eyes at this.

"Father, I am not little anymore; I am seventeen."

"Zaferia, you shall always be my little princess even when you bear your own children." I choose not to reply to this. Children – I am too young to think of such things, honestly.

"Mother, you look beautiful today."

Mother seems quiet and pale this morning. "I am well, daughter."

Hmm, not like Mother at all. Something is wrong.

"May I be excused from the castle after breakfast?"

My mother looks straight at my father. *Odd.*

"Zaferia, you will refrain from going through the forest as of this moment."

5

I look to my father, shocked. "But Father, how will I get to the waterfall?"

He sighs. "You shall no longer visit the waterfall; it has been deemed unsafe."

"But—"

"Zaferia, as your king I forbid you to visit that place. Do not argue with me or disobey me."

I look down at my plate. Something is not right. I sneak a glance at my mother, who is also looking to her plate. "Yes, Father, I will not disobey you as my king."

I want to cry, but I do not, as it is a sign of weakness in a princess. I excuse myself, looking at my mother as I pass her. She has not touched her food. Her eyes are glossy. I put my shoulders back and turn to look ahead. "I am sorry, Zaferia," she says, "I cannot argue with your father on this."

I run to my room, looking at the floor the whole time, fighting back the tears. "Liza, what is going on? Why have I been forbidden to return to my waterfall?"

Liza looks towards the floor. "My lady, I am sorry; I do not know the reason."

Why is my friend lying to me? What is going on? "I shall go to the gardens alone, Liza. It hurts me that you would lie to me."

"My lady, I have been sworn to secrecy. I cannot tell you. Please, Zaferia, do not make me disobey the king."

In the years I have been asking Liza to call me by my name, she never has until today.

Confused, I make my way to my chair in the garden at my favourite spot, which is surrounded by lavender and any other kind of herb and flower you can think of. Listening to the bees busy doing their work, I breathe in all the different scents and ponder what has been said to me, what is going on. I am still treated like a mere child, being forbidden to return to the waterfall. Why, I have been going there since infancy; it has always been safe. *The man from my dreams – is he the reason? He has been coming to the waterfall for only a week, never venturing far from the trees and always appearing briefly, as if to let me know he waits for me.*

Excitement builds up in me with these thoughts as I race from the palace gardens to the exit of the castle. The guards stand in my way, making me stop with such a force I nearly fall over. "I'm sorry, princess you are not allowed to leave the palace," one of them says.

"Excuse me?" Shocked, I look from one guard to the other.

"The king has forbidden it."

"I am only forbidden to enter the forest; the king only required that of me." Oddly the guards look straight ahead and don't reply. Sighing, I turn around and head back to my seat in the garden, touching all the delicate flowers along the way.

Glancing up I notice Liza is running straight for me. *Odd, Liza does not run.* I move to stand up, but Liza reaches me before I reach my full height.

"My lady," she gasps, placing her hand to her chest trying to control her breathing.

"Liza, get your breath and then continue." Her chest is rising and falling so quickly I look at her with concern. "My father and mother, are they well?"

Liza shakes her head. "My lady, y … your father he saw you trying to leave the castle. He is furious that you disobeyed him. You must come at once; he has beckoned you." I follow, trying to keep up with Liza's pace.

"Liza, you must slow down, I am not wearing the appropriate attire for this … this speed." Liza is now dragging me into the palace, towards the throne room. All those within appear startled and bow their heads. *This is so not good.*

Liza stands ramrod straight in front of the guards. I notice they have full armour on. "Open the doors; the king awaits the princess." *This is so not good. Why do the doors always look so threatening?* The guards open the doors, and I am tempted to run in the opposite direction. Liza grabs me and pushes me into the room.

The guards shut the doors in almost a slam; ahead in his throne chair is my father. I look to the left and notice all the curtains are open, allowing the light to hit the stone floor. The fire is bright. Looking to the right I notice the advisors are not at their tables. Ahead of me I notice they are not at the round table either. My father is wearing his royal cloak and crown; I notice the sun hitting the jewels as they sparkle, and I gulp, slowing my pace. "Father," I say nervously, reaching the bottom step of three from his chair.

"Zaferia, princess of Caturn, you will step forward." I gulp, but I approach my father. I go down on one knee and look at the floor. "Zaferia, I forbade you to enter the forest. Not even five minutes after I made this request, you were running off the palace grounds. Explain why you disobeyed your king."

CHAPTER 3

I glance up. "Red" does not describe the colour of my father's face. "Father, I meant no disrespect. You stated for me not to enter the forest or visit the waterfall; I did not realise you meant I was not allowed to leave the safety of the palace. For this I am sorry. I beg for your forgiveness."

My father reaches for my face; his own face softens as he sits on the third step. "Zaferia, you do not need to beg for forgiveness. As a king, I do not need to justify my reasons; as a father, I should have explained." I look at my father puzzled and see a look of protection and concern. I stand; my father remains seated on the step. "Zaferia, you do not know about the meetings I have with mages and high council. I have been trying, as your father, to protect you. As a king, I tried to rule you; for this I am sorry."

The king apologising? What is going on? I try to not look curious, but mages, high council – I know nothing of such things.

"I don't know how to put this as a father. Your life is in danger. A man has been ordered to end your life. This unknown man has been spotted watching you at the waterfall daily for a week."

The man with the blue eyes – could it be? He didn't appear to want to harm me. Did the guards and Liza see him?

"This is why you are forbidden from entering the forest alone. This was unfair of me. I should have posted you my sovereign guards so that you could still visit your place for thinking."

I dare to ask, "Father, you mean I may go back?"

Father looks at me as though he is having an inner battle. "Yes, princess, you may go back, but only with sovereign guards."

I throw myself at him. "Thank you for allowing me to go back. I promise I will not leave without the guards. May I ask which guards?"

My father gazes at me with a knowing look. "Zaferia, you will have Luka, Ivan, and Rogue guarding you."

I look at my father, shocked. "But Father, they are your guards!"

He takes my hands in his. "Only the best for my daughter. They are trained well and will keep what is precious to me safe with their lives. They are outside the door waiting for you."

I give my father a hug and kiss his cheek "Thank you, Father. I will not stray from the guards. Father, you spoke of meetings with mages and higher council; may I ask what you meant?" I imagine all the higher council sitting at the round table with their mages standing behind them in their cloaks, their heads hooded.

Father looks at me, full of pride. "You are aware of a mage's powers, what they can foresee. It is why we have been at peace for so long. Other lands have mages, but ours is the strongest and most loyal. The higher council comprises those in line for the throne or who are already kings from other lands; we meet every full moon to discuss the lands, the people, and the mages' predictions. This past meeting is the first where all the mages saw a threat on your life ending with your death."

Did I just hear my father say all the mages predicted my life coming to an end? Does that mean there has been a threat predicted by one mage or a few? How many times have the guards stopped my life being taken? I look at my father, alarmed. "You mean to tell me that my death has been predicted many times? If so, what makes this time different, and why do all the mages compared to one or two make any difference? I do not understand."

My father looks at me, contemplating his next line. "It is the way it is. It is how it works. All the mages have never been wrong. This is all I can say, Zaferia." He looks to the door. I have been dismissed.

"I shall see you at lunch, Father."

"Be safe, my child." He watches her walk away, praying his guards will not fail him.

****

I wake up to the light hurting my eyes and groan. I ache all over. Realising I am not in my own bed, I sit up quickly again. My side hurts, and

I put my hand there and find blood on it. I go dizzy. I close my eyes and try to compose myself until my head stops spinning. I realise I am not tired any more. Ever so slowly I open my eyes and gasp. The man from my dreams, who is but a foot away, is watching me. "My lady, forgive me," he says.

Looking at him, I wonder what he is going to do next, but all that comes out of my mouth is "You hurt me." Then I charge at him, hitting his chest. It feels as if I'm hitting a brick wall, and I fall to the floor crying. He picks me up, and my whole body freezes. He places me gently back on the bed. My breathing is now getting erratic, and I'm panicking. I start to sweat. "Where am I? Who are you? Where are my guards? Why did you take me?" I look at him, trying to get control of my breathing. "You didn't hurt them, did you?" He chuckles, and it sounds almost like he is purring. I shake my head and tell myself to get a grip. My breathing is more controlled now.

"My lady, please calm down or you will pass out again." My ears perk up at this.

"Again?" I ask, shocked.

"Yes, my lady, you passed out at the waterfall. If not for the fact I had my arm around you, you would have drowned."

Blushing, I look at him. "Impossible; I have never done so!" He stands and starts walking towards me. I push myself further up against the bed.

"My lady, have you ever had a knife at your side and had a strange man take you from your land?"

I blurt out, "You are no stranger, sir. Hang on ... wait ... from my land – where am I?" realising what I have said, I turn as red as a ruby.

He raises an eyebrow. "I am no stranger, you say, for I have only been watching you from a distance for a mere week. Do you know me from somewhere else, Princess?"

Blushing yet again, I push my shoulders back and chin up. "My father will seek you out and kill you. Release me at once y ... you brute!"

He looks at me with a glint in his eye, puts his head back, and laughs loudly. *Who is this man? How dare he kidnap a princess in front of the guards!* "Oh no," I whisper to myself, "He will kill the guards."

He stops laughing, and the next thing I know, he is nose-to-nose with me. "My lady, your guards are already dead – an honourable death, for the king would have killed them for not keeping you out of harm's way."

Looking straight into his beautiful eyes, I managed to whisper out "Liza?" While waiting for his next words, I try to control my breathing.

"Alive, for I shall harm no woman unless she harms me."

He smells divine – fresh water and a smell I cannot figure out. I am grateful that my friend is still alive. "What is your name?" My speech comes out in a way I have never heard it, and it confuses me.

I was right; his skin feels like the finest of silk. Nose-to-nose, I want to kiss him. Suddenly he moves and I feel as red as a ruby. *Did he realise I wanted to kiss him?*

"My name is not important, princess. What is important – and the question you should be asking – is why have I taken you?" With that he walks out and locks the door. I look at that door for what seems like ten minutes with my mouth hanging open. Throwing myself back to lie down, I ask myself what that was and why I had those thoughts. *Is this the path that has been chosen for me?* Confused, I wrinkle my nose, realising the mages said my life was in danger. Not one, but all of them, had this premonition. I curl into a ball and weep.

****

In the throne room, Drakus looks to his guard. "Theolis, stand guard at our guest's room and return to me when the cook has prepared lunch for two in the great grand room. Also, Marcus will not hear of her arrival; he will sense her soon enough." Shocked, Theolis bows to his king, exiting backwards. When he gets to the room, he hears distinct sniffles. *Oh, my great king, what have you done?* Dropping into his throne, Drakus wonders how he will get out of this quandary. The king of Caturn will surely start a war upon his land; after all, he has kidnapped their only child. He did not intend to kidnap her, but the thought of someone hurting his true love was too much for him to bear. He is determined to treat Zaferia as his queen; she will wear the finest of clothes. He wonders, had she dreamed of him as he of her? *She smells of lavender.* He wants to kiss her, but he realises she would hate him for taking her. But her skin feels like the finest of silks; her touch is electrifying. *Does she feel it too?* Sighing, he retires to his room.

At lunch he waits for Zaferia. She never comes, so he requests food be sent to her room, which is sent back. *Stubborn woman; I must show her I mean her no harm.*

****

Sleep did not come easy for me last night; having a guard posted outside my door made me mad. Why would I escape? I don't even know where I am. Eventually I fell asleep watching the moon and stars. Looking from the bed when I awake, I realise I'm in the most beautiful room I have ever seen; the finest of materials are draped over the windows and doorways. The're is also a drape hiding the main door. The furniture is a deep mahogany. There is a desk in the corner and a lavish rug so thick it tickles my toes. Looking down, I realise it is made of sheep's wool. The fire is surrounded by a beautiful mantel with different shapes and styles of candlestick holders. A long mirror close to the main door mesmerises me, sparkling with rubies and every jewel known to man. Touching the edge of the mirror before looking into it, I gasp in alarm. "My, I'm a mess. I need a bath and clean clothes." Turning around, I notice there are no drapes on the bed. There is a light tapping at the door before it slowly opens. "I come in peace, my lady." Recognising his voice straight away, with sheer panic I grab a candlestick, hold it above my head, and hit him.

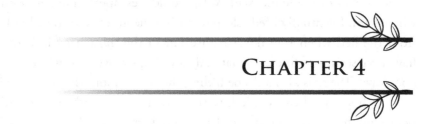

CHAPTER 4

Drakus hits the floor with a loud thud. "Oh my goodness, I have killed him." I hesitate a moment and then reach down to see if he is still breathing. "Thank God!" I drop the holder and flee the room, but I freeze when I reach the stairwell. I then run along the entryway, nearly knocking over a vase of mixed roses. Finally I open the front door and slam it shut again. "Who keeps a dragon at their front door?" I shout. Hearing a loud groan, I run to my left, where I see a lot of draped material. *Maybe there is a hidden room,* I think. I knock my legs against some furniture as I move along. A light would be very helpful right now, but I manage to get to the drapes, touching the walls and hoping to find a door.

****

Drakus is not happy. He hopes Zeva scared the life out of her when he hears her scream. He starts running down to the stairs just in case. When he opens the front door, Zeva motions left. Drakus locks the door. "Oh Princess, there is no escape, for the dragon can sense you." He starts walking left through the grand hall, lighting candles on the mantel. The mirror above lights the whole room up.

****

"Know this, my lady; you shall never raise an arm to me again … if you want to see your land again."

"You dare threaten me, brute?" I slowly start walking towards him.

Drakus's temper softens. "Come, my lady; I shall introduce you to Zeva."

I raise an eyebrow. "Zeva?" As I reach Drakus, I realise I am breathing quicker the closer I get to him. I give him a confused look as he takes my arm and walks towards the front door.

Opening the door, I release my breath, which comes out in a gush, reddening my cheeks. Before me stands the most beautiful dragon I have ever seen. The gold is breath-taking, but when Zeva moves I see a glimmer of reds and purples. Her scales show perfection. Looking up to Zeva, I realise her eyes are pure green. The dragon bows her head, and so do I.

****

Drakus finds this meeting exceptional, as he has never seen a dragon bow to anyone. He looks at Zaferia and finds at that moment that she takes his breath away. His heart feels as though it has stopped beating. He notices she is moving towards Zeva, and he releases her arm. *Why does she not run from him? Is she maybe gaining the dragons' trust?*

****

Why's this brute's touch so powerful, and why do I crave it so?

"He is no brute, my princess, but the man who has spent many a night in your dreams."

I look to my captor, then at the dragon, and finally my surroundings. I wonder, *Who just spoke to me?* All I can see is land and trees.

"It is I, Zeva, who speaks to you."

My mouth drops. "Dragon Zeva, I am wondering how you are capable of talking to me. Does the man from my dreams hear us?" I look at Drakus, noticing he is watching her intently.

"Princess, he knows not what we say. I choose who can hear me. With you it is an honour." Zeva lowers her head, bowing.

I return my eyes to the dragon. "What is my dream man's name?"

Zeva looks straight at me. "It is not for me to say, Princess."

This makes me grunt.

"She is magnificent, br—"

"My name is Drakus, my lady."

15

As I gaze at him, my heart actually stops beating. "D … Drakus, why am I here?"

Drakus appears to be saddened by this question. "It is time for lunch, Zaferia."

I frown at this and look down and then back up to meet his dreamy eyes. "I am not in suitable attire for lunch, nor clean enough. I seem to have missed my evening bath for some odd reason."

He smiles and places his hand on my arm. "Was it some brute who kidnapped you, my lady?"

I look in his eyes and see he is smiling with his eyes. I like that. "Yes, a brute indeed." With that he closes the front door. I notice he doesn't lock it. The glass in the front door is of various colours.

"I will call the maids to attend to you at once, my lady," says Drakus. "Is there anything in particular you desire?"

I grin. "Fresh lavender, if this is possible in your land?" There is no hostility in my response.

"It will be done." I reluctantly step forward and turn around, blushing as I do so. "I made haste in my departure; where is my room?"

Drakus makes his way to me and leads me to my room. The candlestick is where I dropped it. I grimace. "I am sorry for hitting you. Thank you for returning me to my room." He picks up the candlestick and hands it back to me with one eye raised. I take it from him looking only at it. "Until lunch is served, Drakus."

He knows he has been dismissed. "Yes, my lady, see you shortly." He walks away smiling.

Closing the door, sighing deeply, I am smiling and feeling all in a flutter. A light tap lets me know that the maids have arrived. When I open the door, the smell of lavender hits me. "Come in," I say, placing the holder back on the mantle following the maids. Never have I worn such a red before; my eyes stand out and as I twirl, watching the skirt spin. It looks beautiful. Nervously I make my way to the dinner hall. I have never felt so happy and nervous at the same time. The clothing feels like a second skin; it is made from the finest of silks.

****

I find Drakus waiting for me in the dining hall. He sits at the head of the table, expecting I will be sat at the opposite end; but he pulls out the chair next to his, bowing in thanks. "My lady, dinner shall be served within the minute." I sit with my hands in my lap, unsure as to what to say, noticing the setting is of the finest materials and best-looking dishware I have ever seen. The utensils all look like gold. I gaze at him, puzzled. "Drakus, who are you?"

He seems to ponder for a moment before answering. "I am king. My lady." My mouth drops open. "YOU. ARE. KING?– yet you dare to defy the peace treaty and kidnap me from my land. A king. Such a noble man you are."

A starter is placed in front of me, yet all I see is red. When the servants don't leave, I turn to them. "Leave this room at once." They look at Drakus and he nods. They leave. I rise from my seat. "Excuse me, my *king*; I seem to have lost my appetite."

I go back to my room, slamming the door behind me and screaming from the top of my lungs. I notice a flash go past the window, so I run and jump straight out. Zeva just manages to get under me in time. "Fly as fast as you can."

Zeva says to Drakus, "Do not worry, my king; we will not go far."

From his seat at the table he replies, "Very well, keep her safe from harm. Remember, someone means to harm her."

Zeva growls and releases fire. "Not on my watch."

I feel euphoric. Never before have I felt so free as I do with the wind in my hair, on the back of a fire-breathing dragon. My anger dissipates as I watch the land beneath me: the grass moving in the wind, the trees moving from the slight breeze. The air smells so fresh, and I notice farmers in the pastures with their horses.

"I sensed your feelings and knew you needed me, my queen."

Shocked, I nearly lose my grip. "I am not queen; I am Princess of Caturn."

"You are my queen. I serve you and my king."

Oh, how I wish Liza were here.

Zeva turns. "Where are we going?"

"We shall fetch her, my queen."

I laugh. "How do you know I will not run into the castle and shout 'dragon' from the top of my voice?"

Zeva laughs. "You belong with the king now, my queen."

We spend the rest of the way to my homeland in silence. When we arrive, the sun has well and truly set, and darkness is growing. Zeva lands on the palace wall just above Liza's window. "I shall fly around."

I reach for her. "Wait; do not fly around, for the guards shall see you. I have a hidden wall. I shall meet you over there; it will be safe."

Zeva nods. "Very well. I shall see you soon, my queen."

CHAPTER 5

I make it quietly to Liza's room and wake her up by covering her mouth to stifle the scream. "Shh! You will alert the guards. Come with me." Liza quickly puts some clothes on and follows me without question.

When we reach the end of the treeline, Liza sees the dragon and freezes and starts screaming. Zeva grimaces. "My queen, we must hurry; the guards will have heard her scream."

I grab Liza and drag her towards the dragon. "Be quiet and help me get you on; the guards will hurt Zeva because of your screaming."

Liza looks at the dragon and closes her mouth. "I'm sorry." Liza gets on, and I mount in front of her and ask her to loosen her grip so I can breathe. We take off towards Drakus.

"My queen, thank you." Taken aback, I ask, "Whatever for, Zeva?"

"For returning to your king."

Smiling, I kiss Zeva's head. "You are very welcome, Zeva." All the time, Liza is clinging onto me for dear life. *I am going to have bruises.*

****

"My king, we are home," I say when we arrive. Sighing with relief, he walks into the room to encounter a high-pitched scream that nearly deafens him. "Liza, hush at once and bow to the great king of … of … Drakus, where am I?"

"You are in Falor, my queen," Zeva replies.

"Thank you, Zeva. Liza – the great king of Falor."

Drakus frowns at Zeva. "What did you do?"

"My king, I simply took the queen to fetch her confidante."

"You took her home!" Drakus pales.

"My king, I returned."

"Why did you return? You could have gotten Zeva harmed in Caturn."

I place my hand on his face. "But my king, I returned. As Zeva placed her trust in me, I could not go against that faith."

"King of Falor, it is, erm … an honour, I think. My lady, is this your kidnapper?" looking at Drakus, I simply reply, "Yes."

"My king, is the chamber next to mine available?"

"Yes. Would you like the chamber for Liza prepared?" He looks back to me.

"That would be fantastic, if you could."

He looks at me, puzzled.

"My lady, a word if I may," says Liza.

"In due time, Liza. Drakus, will you escort me to the gardens, please?"

Automatically he reaches for my arm, and we walk towards the gardens. The smell of honeysuckle and lavender hits me. Once there, it dawns on him what happened. "I need to sit, my lady."

Looking at him, I say, "I do not know where the seating area is."

He looks confused at this, then realises I have never been in the gardens before. "Oh." He starts walking towards the chairs. Once seated, he turns to face me. I sit up straight. He notices I am ready for his questions.

"My lady, you take my dragon, return to your castle for Liza, and then return to me through the trust of a dragon?"

I look at him, shocked at his question. "The trust of a dragon is a sacred thing, my king. I would not tarnish such a gift." He sits there not knowing what to say next, and I sigh. "In my chamber I was furious. I saw Zeva flying past, and I just jumped out of the window. I …"

He grabs my arm and turns me to face him. "You did what! How did you know Zeva would catch you? What if you had fallen to your death? How did you not know I wouldn't kill you on your return?"

A tiny giggle escapes my lips. "My king, do you honestly distrust your dragon?"

Drakus almost growls as this. "That is not what I asked," he says through gritted teeth.

I look at him seriously. "Zeva did not want me to suffer any more than I had. I wish to retire for the night."

He looks at me, shocked. No one has ever spoken to him in such a manner.

"Also, I would like to visit the gardens in the morning, as they smell sublime." He leaves without a word, taking me back to the castle, and goes in search of Marcus.

****

Not five minutes after I enter my room, Liza runs in.

"My lady, what an earth is going on? You drag me from my slumber, put me on a dragon, and drag me across lands. My lady, we thought you were dead."

"The guards, are they alive?"

Liza sighs, looking sad. "Ivan and Luka are dead, my lady. Rogue is alive but in a bad way. He wishes himself dead. The king is furious with him for thinking this way. Rogue will be up and about in no time."

"What about you, Liza; how did you fare?"

Liza turned red. "I failed you, my lady; I am so sorry. I awoke on the floor. I passed out, and when I came to I found Rogue on the edge of the pool, trying to get out. My lady, he was crying; he kept saying 'Fe'." I smile, as Liza does not know his nickname for me. Liza rises. "Zaferia, tell me about this kidnapper who has won your heart and how he did so." With that we get into the bed.

Once in a comfortable position, I relay what happened from when I woke to the time of getting into bed. "When shall we be going home, my lady?"

"I do not know, Liza; I am content here."

"My lady, the king and queen are sick with worry; please return with me even for just a day."

I stared at Liza, realising she was right. "Zeva ..."

"My queen."

"Can you hear me no matter where I am?"

"Yes, my queen."

"Very well. Liza, we shall return home tomorrow, but I shall return to my king the very next day. I just need to tell Drakus. He will not be pleased. As he is king, we cannot say he was my captor, as my Father will declare war. I shall tell him of our plans in the morning after I have visited the gardens." With this we fall asleep together. It feels like old times sharing a bed with Liza.

The gardens are breathtaking; never have I seen such a vast collection of flowers. Most I don't even recognise, but they smell beautiful. I notice the birds chirping and bees buzzing from flower to flower. After sighing and then allowing a smile, feeling content here, I turn and go back to my room. "Liza, remain here. I shall send a maid up with breakfast."

"Very well, my lady."

I make my way downstairs, taking in deep breaths to calm my nerves. *This is going to be hard, sitting in same seat as last night.* I look to him.

"My lady, did you sleep well?" he asks.

"Yes, my king." Drakus asks me my thoughts on the palace gardens and seems happy with my reply. I then hesitate, taking a deep breath. "Drakus, why did you take me?" He looks down to his plate again. "Please, Drakus, tell me."

"My lady, your life had been threatened. All the mages predicted it. I didn't want this to happen. I am not the one to kill you; I must merely protect you until the threat passes."

"Drakus, I shall return home with Liza—"

"You can't, my lady; the predictions—"

"Let me finish, my king."

He looks at her. "Yes, my apologies."

"I shall return home today with Liza. I shall return in twenty-four hours; Zeva will hear my call and pick me up, as I do not know the way by horse or on foot."

Drakus looks at me with his mouth open.

"I take it, my king that it is okay that I return, from the silence and look on your face."

Drakus closes his mouth. "But why would you return here?"

"I shall answer another day. Come, let's eat; then we shall be on our way."

****

Drakus watches as Zeva fades into the distance. "She will return, my king." He hopes so, because right now he feels as though letting them go was the wrong decision. "Stay close; kill anyone that harms her." Drakus hates letting Zaferia go; it pains him knowing he cannot protect her at the waterfall. The death of the soldiers pains him greatly, and he hated killing them, especially the one she called Rogue. He feels he would give anything to take back their deaths. He walks back into the castle, tempted to ride a horse for the first time in years, but he trusts Zaferia to come back. He notices that the sun is almost high in the sky. He would love to watch a sunset with Zaferia in his arms.

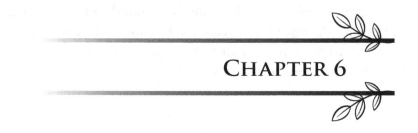

CHAPTER 6

"Drop us off at the waterfall. I do not wish to see you harmed."

"Yes, my queen. I will fly high to make sure you get to the castle safely." I nod. "As you wish, Zeva." I have been missing the waterfall badly. Once Zeva drops us off, we sit for a few minutes.

"My lady, who do we say took you, and how did we escape?"

"My dear Liza, I have been thinking about that one. I have brought the clothes Drakus took me in. I shall change into them here. As for you, we shall rip your clothes and smear mud on us. By the time we reach the castle, it will have dried."

"Clever, my lady; very clever."

We soon arrive at the castle caked in mud. The king runs through the palace with his wife behind him. "Zaferia," he says, hugging so tightly I think my bones will break.

"Father, I have missed you." I look to my mother; her eyes are full of tears. I throw myself at her. "Mother, oh how I have missed you. I love you both so much. The guards—"

"Zaferia, Luka and Ivan were killed protecting you."

I look to Liza. "We shall give them an honourable funeral, Father. What of Rogue?"

"Yes, my little princess, we shall. Rogue is healing. He will be glad to see you; you will be his reason to live again."

I walk towards the castle in the arms of my parents; Liza follows. "Father, may we retire to my room to bathe, then meet up in the throne room to discuss what happened? Also, could I see Rogue?"

I look to my father; pride is written all over his face. "Yes, daughter, we shall meet in the throne room; Rogue shall be happy to see you."

Once Liza and I are in the bathroom, we go over the story again. "Liza, remember, you sneaked away from the castle; I found you on the way home. Do not slip up on this."

"Yes, my lady. Now jump in the bath."

"Liza, may I suggest we wash together over the bath? I think we went over the top with the mud, and I fear we will look worse getting out of the bath." We look at each other and laugh.

Seeing Rogue is emotional. The moment he sees me, he shoots out of bed and hugs me so tight I can't breathe; then he puts me at arm's distance and starts checking me for any marks. "Rogue, I am well; how are you?"

He hugs me again. "Fe, I was so scared for you. I failed you and the king; I am so sorry, Fe."

I hug him tighter and place my head on his chest. "I'm home now, Ro, safe, and I have never been so happy to see the bossiest man in my life."

He laughs. "It's good to have you home, Fe. How did you escape your captor?"

I shrug. "I hit him with a candlestick holder just ran till I bumped into Liza, and here we are."

He hugs me again.

"Ro, I most go and see my father and mother. You need to rest so that you can boss me about again." We both laugh at this.

"Anything for my little Fe."

I give him a kiss on the cheek and start walking to the throne room while fighting back tears, grateful he is not dead. On getting to the throne room, I find that Liza is there waiting for me. "You ready, Zaferia?"

I nod. She looks to the guards. "Open the doors."

The guards nod. "Welcome home, Princess," says one of them. "Girl's, we took the liberty of bringing food in; we thought you might both be hungry."

"Thank you," we both say at the same time.

It is some time later that we return to my room with full bellies and satisfied parents. "Do you think they believed us, Liza?"

"I believe so. You told a very compelling story, telling your father we came from the North. My lady, you will be returning to Drakus tomorrow; how will we explain that?"

"I will be coming of age to marry soon, Liza; I hope my king asks my father."

I walk to the window and shift my attention. "Zeva."

"Yes, my queen."

Looking for her, I notice a small dot in the sky above me. "Will you return me to our king and have me back here before sunrise?"

"Yes, my queen. Our king is not expecting us till tomorrow, though."

"Then, my dear dragon, we shall surprise him."

****

Drakus hears the beating of wings. Thinking the worst, he is just about to start running for the door. "My king, all is well. Our queen has an idea but must return before the sunrise." He still runs to the door. His sweet Zaferia has returned. He opens the door in time for Zaferia to slide to the ground. She looks like a jewel to cherish. He clears his throat. "Is all well, my lady?"

****

I walk to him. "Yes, my king, all is well. May I have a moment of your time?"

He smiles sweetly at me. "You may have all the time you desire, my lady."

Once seated at the table, I place myself opposite of him, removing him from the head of the table. He looks shocked at the seating arrangement. "My king, what I have to discuss must be face-to-face; it is of the greatest importance."

He looks at me. "My king, you have turned a deathly white; do not panic." I ask for all the courses to come at once, telling the maids that I will serve the food to their king. He nods in agreement, mostly out of fascination at a princess handing him his food. This was one for the books.

"My king."

"Hmm."

Speaking a bit more firmly, I change my tone. "Drakus, look at me."

"I am sorry, but I find it fascinating you want to serve me food."

I roll my eyes at this. "Drakus, listen to me. It is important that you do so."

He looks up. "Sorry, my lady, you have my attention."

"Very well. Listen and listen wisely. I will be coming of age in a month to legally marry any man that my father approves of. Will you come to the castle to ask me to be your queen?"

On hearing this, Drakus rises and summons Zeva. "Take Zaferia home."

"My king, you have turned a nasty shade of green. I have failed to please your appetite."

He looks at her. "No, Zaferia, you have not failed with the food; you are going home for good."

Looking up at him, shocked, I drop my spoon and its contents onto the table. "My king, I thought you wanted me here with you."

"No, leave at once, Zaferia; leave now."

I hold back my tears. "No, this is my home now – here with you. I am your queen. I beg of you, do not send me away."

Drakus drags me to Zeva and pushes me onto her. "Zeva, leave now." I try getting off, but Zeva takes me home, with me crying into her neck. Zeva is furious with her king and is determined he will know about it too, king or not.

****

Drakus is fuming. He can't understand why he loves Zaferia and yet he still sent her away, breaking both their hearts. *How could I marry her? The moment I step foot on Caturn I will be killed on the spot for kidnapping and murdering sovereign guards.*

Instead, he waits for war to be declared on his land. "Zeva," he says, "prepare the dragons for war."

Zeva just turns her back to him. "I will do no such thing, my king." She turns, ready to fly off.

"Zeva, do not turn you're back on me, for I am your king."

Zeva stops, turns, and walks towards him, startling him. "King? You do not deserve that title; nor do you deserve us. I. AM. QUEEN Drakus; I serve no one." With that she flies off high into the sky, breathing fire.

Drakus looks to the floor, sighing. *Even my dragon has turned on me.* He walks into the castle.

CHAPTER 7

As I climb into my room, tears stream down my face. Liza runs to me, worried I will fall. I land on Liza with a grunt and then more tears. Liza looks up to see Zeva breathing fire and making a lot of noise. "My lady, what happened? Please talk to me," she asks as she strokes my hair, saying calm, soothing words in my ear.

The crying eventually eases as the sun starts setting. "I told him m … m … my plans. He threw me out, Liza, just like that."

"Oh Zaferia, I am so, so sorry. What shall we do?"

At this I sit up. "I shall marry no one. My heart is broken; it will turn into ice. No man will have the right to touch me."

Liza looks at me, shocked. "You will not be permitted to do so, for if your father realises this, he shall force a husband on you, and you shall be forever trapped. Drakus may have a good reason for doing what he did, my lady; please do not give up on love, for it shines so brightly on the both of you." At this I start crying again.

Liza dismisses us both from breakfast. "You must stop crying, my lady. Your parents will wonder what is wrong."

Looking up at Liza, I reply, "I have been kidnapped. They will see this as the stress from that."

Liza manages to get Zaferia to bed and stays with her all night.

I am in my morning bath when Liza enters the room. "My lady, you should have woken me; I would have run your bath."

Looking up at Liza, I say, "There is no need; you looked so peaceful I let you sleep." Getting out of the bath, I reach for my robe. Liza runs to grab it, and I laugh. "Oh, my good friend, where would I be without you?"

"You would be where you are now, my lady." Liza say's with a smile

I join my parents for breakfast. I can tell my father is looking at me, and I hope he does not see that the sparkle from my eyes is gone and in its place is sadness. This will tear at his heart, and I know he will call an emergency meeting with the high council and mages and declare war on the brute that took his daughter.

Later on in the day I decide to go to my favourite spot in the garden. I sit in my favourite chair, thinking of Drakus and how much I long to be with him. *I don't understand why he sent me away. I thought he—*

"Zaferia, Zaferia, you must come quickly!" I get up with a confused look on my face.

"Liza, what is wrong?"

"It's your father; he has declared war on Tenalp we only said the North, Zaferia, they are innocent, yet the servants state they saw you there. We must do something."

I run with Liza to the palace. "Father, why have you declared war on Tenalp?"

The king looks at me and simply says, "Because I am king."

Shocked, I say, "Oh, because you are king. What did they do to break the treaty?"

"Yes, they broke the treaty not just because of you; you will never dare question my actions again, child." He walks away, leaving me frozen to the spot. Liza comes and drags me away.

I pace my room. "My lady," says Liza, "you will end up going through the floor if you continue—"

I turn to Liza. "Yes, all is well. My father is going to war with innocent people through my fault alone. I will be a murderer, and he will not even listen. Oh Liza, what will I do? I could stand for Tenalp against my father, but will that prevail?"

Liza says nothing.

****

Over lunch with my mother and father, I ask about the war on Tenalp. "Hush, child, no sort of discussion shall be discussed whilst we are eating," says the king.

I find the courage. "I do not wish you to go to war. We have lived in peace for so long, and I am back unharmed; please reconsider."

Shocked, the king looks at to his daughter. '*Yes. She will make a good queen for her courage and beliefs are strong*' "My daughter, I am glad you are back unharmed, but Tenalp broke the treaty. This was not seen by the mages, and the king of Tenalp says he had no knowledge of your presence on his land but understands the reasons I go to war with him. I have been generous and given him a month to prepare."

I look at my father with tears streaming down my face. "Then I stand with Tenalp, for I do not agree with this war. We are good people, and our hearts are strong and full of love; why tarnish them with hatred? Your people have looked up to you for as long as you have been king; now you bring them death. They will turn on you."

With this I stand and move to leave, with Father demanding my return and Mother crying into her starter. I quickly place my hand on her shoulder as I walk past her, fighting back my own emotions. Yes what I am doing feels right to me, but not to my parents.

After walking straight out of the castle, I start walking towards the field before I can be stopped. "Zeva, I will meet you in the field."

Zeva replies straight away. "Yes, my queen."

Walking past the guards at the gate, I walk to the field just as Zeva lands. "Oh Zeva, I have missed you; let's fly over the land towards Tenalp." Looking shocked, Zeva agrees. In the air, I lean to look down over Tenalp. No preparations are being made for war; I am confused. "Zeva, land."

"I am sorry, my queen, but I cannot."

"Why can you not land?"

"I'm sorry, my queen; the king would never allow me to put you in intentional danger I protect you with my life." I feel so touched at this. Thinking of Drakus, I smile.

I remember the crystals. "Very well, take me to the edge of the forest. I wish to visit my waterfall." Once at the waterfall, knowing Zeva is flying overhead, I dive into the water. It is slightly warm. Grabbing a crystal, I get out of the water and sit on the edge with my feet dangling in the water, watching the ripples my feet make, debating whether I should go home and face my father yet again in the throne room. I am curious as to why he never has any advisors present at these meetings.

31

Rustling breaks my thoughts. I turn in time to see nothing but blackness. Waking to an unfamiliar noise, I try to move, but I quickly realise my hands and feet have been tied and a cloth has been tied across my mouth, stopping me from speaking. I try calling for Zeva but receive no reply. I start panicking. I try to sit up, only to fall back down. *Am I in a carriage of some sort?* It feels like it's moving, but it is a strange-looking one. After what feels like forever it comes to a stop. I try to force myself into a corner, preparing to be out of reach, but the door opens too quickly and I notice there are bars between me and the man on the outside. "Ah, Princess, call all you like; your dragon will not hear you."

I look at him, puzzled.

"I have placed a spell on the carriage; no one shall hear your screams, or see us."

Still looking at him, it dawns at me I'm going to die. He looks so familiar, but I cannot place where I have seen him before. If his hood weren't causing a shadow, I would be able to get a better look.

"Your father, the king, is a fool to go to war with Tenalp. But do not worry; he shall die by my hand alone, as shall you." With this I allow the tears to fall. He closes the door, and the carriage starts moving again.

****

Zeva doesn't sense Zaferia's presence and flies lower, but Zaferia is no longer at the waterfall. "My king, I can no longer sense Zaferia." Zeva flies lower, searching but finding nothing.

"Search high and low for her, Zeva. Do not rest until you find her!."

Zeva searches all night, sensing nothing.

****

The king storms into Liza's room, scaring her half to death. "Liza, where is my daughter?"

"My king, I have not seen her since before lunch."

At this the king roars for his guards. "Search the palace, gardens, and the waterfall for my daughter. If you do not find her, search further afield. Glador – where is that mage? I demand your presence now."

As soon as the king speaks, Glador appears. "Yes, my king."

Turning, the king says, "Where is my daughter?"

The mage starts walking along the corridor. "My king, I have lost her spirit. It seems whoever has taken her does not want her found this time."

The king stops. "This time, Glador?"

The mage looks at him, bemused. "Why yes, I knew where she was before."

At this the king roars, "And you didn't tell me?"

The mage takes hold of the king's arm. "I have tried many spells to locate the princess. They have all failed." He sighs, disappointed with his failure.

"My king, when Zaferia disappeared the first time, this is what she felt." With that he allows the king a moment. "She loves her captor."

This thought sickens and shocks the king.

"No, he was not her captor; he was her protector and true love."

The king, confused, continues walking. "Who is he?"

The mage falls in step with him. "His name is Drakus, king of Falor. He and his dragons will seek out Zaferia." At this point they reach the throne, where the king sits and stews on the mage's words. "Oh, and my king, it is improper to barge into a young woman's room, king or not do not do it again." He then vanished.

The king was too shocked to react; he just sat there. He then stood up abruptly. "I must tell Rogue that she has been kidnapped and protected by a spell where no one can reach her."

"My daughter – where is she, Gladonis?"

The king looks up to see the queen approach him. "My love, she is out of our grasp. Have no fear; her true love will rescue her." The queen silently weeps in the king's arms. All he can think of is how Glador had called him her king. *Her love is undeniable, but how does this Drakus feel for my daughter?*

"Glador," the king states. When he appears, the king says that he wants to meet Drakus.

"It will be done." Glador connects to Marcus. "My king, Gladonis of Caturn requires your assistance and meeting at once."

****

Drakus looks up, shocked that his mage Marcus would disturb him. "When?"

Marcus looks down. "At once, my king."

Drakus looks irritated at this and also alarmed, but he is determined to go to the king with his head held high, as he deserves to die for sending his true love away. He sighs. "Zeva, are you close enough to drop me at Caturn Castle?" There is silence for a while. "Zeva, the king of Caturn requires my presence." Almost straight away, he hears wings.

"Yes, I am by the front door."

With that they took off to Caturn. All the way there, Drakus prepared to die by the hand of his true love's father.

****

I wake up scared, tied to a bed by my hands and feet in a dungeon. My mouth is no longer restricted, so I scream for Zeva until my throat can no longer take the strain. I try breaking out of the ties, but it is no use. I think back to when I was in the wagon and of the magic he said he used. He must have used the same magic, for here I am alone. I start getting scared, and then it dawns on me who my captor is.

CHAPTER 8

Drakus looks at Zaferia's home and is amazed. Ivy climbs the castle walls, and the courtyard is filled with flowers. The scents are so soothing. Closing his eyes, he smells lavender. He opens his eyes, expecting to see her; but he is disappointed, as she is nowhere in sight. His home feels and looks simple. With his head and shoulders down, he arrives at the doors to the castle. Approaching the guard, he states, "Drakus to see king of Caturn."

He walks to the throne room. He has never seen so many paintings or tapestries; he finds it breath-taking. He is dreading seeing the king. The throne room doors look threating enough. Taking a steady breath, he nods to the guard who opens the door. Drakus approaches the king of Caturn on the throne and bows, keeping a comfortable distance. "King Gladonis, you requested my presence."

Gladonis looks at him. "You are the man who stole my daughter's heart." Drakus looks at the king. He is shocked that the king made no mention of his having taking her. "I did not know I had won your daughter's heart; forgive me."

Gladonis is amused with this. "You did not know? For it was in her eyes; any fool could have seen this."

Drakus grits his teeth. "You call me a fool, king?"

"Now, now. I said any fool could see this, not that you are a fool; do not twist my words."

Drakus looks down, feeling ashamed for his outburst. After hesitating, he asks, "Forgive me. How is the princess?" He glances up at the king, hoping she is in her room. But he sees sadness in the king's eyes.

"She has been taken again."

Drakus hesitates. "Taken?"

"Yes, Drakus, taken. Glador, my mage, cannot detect her spirit. We fear witchcraft of a strong kind has taken her and a spell has been cast so that no one can detect her." Gladonis wonders if Glador made him aware of who will find his daughter. He is undecided if he should say. "Will you search for Zaferia, Drakus?"

"Yes. My dragon, Zeva, will not rest till Zaferia is home safe; nor will I." Gladonis looks at Drakus. "I should have you killed for taking her. You may leave now before I change my mind, my daughter may not take it kindly to me killing you."

This shocks Drakus. Turning, he heads towards the doors, noticing no advisors are at their table. "Zeva, we are leaving now."

"Yes, my king. What of my queen?" Drakus does not reply; he just climbs onto her back and they fly back to Falor. The only thing Drakus wants to do is hold Zaferia and never let her go. He decides he will ask for her father's permission to marry her. He will not rest until he finds his queen. He knows that if he had not sent her away, she would still be alive safe. He feels like a fool.

****

"Well, Glador, what did you sense from him?"

Walking out of the shadows, Glador has a bemused look on his face. "My king, he does truly love the princess. However, he feels he is unworthy of such a gift as your daughter now."

The king contemplates these words as Glador vanishes. *It must be guilt that Drakus feels; finding her will vanquish those thoughts.*

Gladonis goes in search of his queen, trusting in his mage completely.

"What of the king of Falor, does he love our daughter as Glador says?" asks the queen, Itisha.

Gladonis walks up to Itisha and holds her in his arms. "My queen, I do believe he will make an excellent match for our daughter." Itisha smiles, knowing that her daughter is going to be well loved. "My queen, he has dragons searching for our daughter, but they cannot sense her; shall we ask the wolves if they can assist?"

The queen looks at her husband. "Yes, my love. Summon the wolf king."

He realises that he should call Glador, but he continues to hold her. "Come, my love, let us retire for the night." Itisha nods, and they walk arm in arm to bed.

****

Tristan is contemplating taking a wife. As alpha, this is expected; plus he will not feel so lonely if he does so. There are plenty of she-wolves to choose from, but they are too submissive. He wants someone who will stand up to him and his wolf.

Glador appears to his left. "King Gladonis of Caturn requires your presence at once." Without explanation, he just vanishes, before Tristan can even muster a growl.

Tristan stands from his throne and starts walking towards his second in command, Damoc. His throne is open to all of his people and is used most of the day. It isn't a grand castle, and the furnishings are of deep mahogany, for they are simple people. There are no pictures or tapestries. Tristan is grateful that there are no mages on his land. Even though he signed the peace treaty, he fought them on that and won.

He realises no one else noticed the mage appear. *Odd.* He gets up and starts walking towards Damoc. Noticing the she-wolves moving out of his way, lowering their heads in submission, he sighs, gritting his teeth. "Damoc, we have been summoned to Caturn by the king; we leave at first light." Not giving his second a chance to reply, he leaves the throne room and goes to his room.

Looking in the mirror, he takes in his appearance. He is muscular and toned well. His hair is light brown, and his eyes brown, which is rare in a wolf. Looking to his stomach, he touches his scar, conjuring the memories of being stabbed by a woman many years before. She is only one who had ever stood up to him. She escaped that night, and he searched for her but never found her. He vowed to kill whoever let her out of the dungeon, using the slowest form of torture. He wants her and only her.

He often dreamt of her crouching on the floor, knife in hand, dripping with his blood; but all he ever saw was her green eyes looking straight at him, showing no sign of fear or remorse. Before he could dream of more, he always woke up sweating.

"She would have made a good alphena." He grins at the thought of the only female to ever take him on.

At first light, he and Damoc change into wolf form and run through forests, rivers, and the long grasses of the lands, resting deep within the forests at night. They reach Caturn on the third day, where they change into clothes the guards give them. "The king would not be pleased with you parading around the grounds and palace naked."

Tristan and Damoc agree and dress. This is their first visit here. Once in the courtyard, they both stop short. The gardens and the palace look intimidating. "Alpha, why have we been summoned?"

"I do not know, Damoc; shall we find out?" With this they walk to the palace doors. Noticing the looks and the whispers from the people around them, they let out a low growl.

CHAPTER 9

The guards stand in front of the doors as straight as Tristan had ever seen. "State your business."

Damoc replies, "Your king sent his mage. Our presence is required immediately. This is the alpha-king Tristan of Atalonia. Notify the king of our arrival." After a few minutes, Tristan and Damoc are shown to the throne room to wait for the king.

Tristan notices that there are the guards at the side doors and no advisors in the room. He frowns at this. A few minutes later the king arrived through a side door, followed by the queen. They take their seats. The queen speaks first. "Tristan, alpha-king of Atalonia, forgive my husband's rash summoning; we should have requested your presence, not demanded it."

Tristan does not know what to say, as he has never heard of a queen speaking before the king, so he nods in response.

"Alpha, our daughter, the princess, has been taken. Our mage, Glador, cannot detect her spirit and feels that a spell has been cast so that no one can seek her out. We ask for your assistance, as your ability to shift into wolf form will help us greatly. We are praying that you will catch her scent. Will you help us?"

As he looks at the queen, he is about to say no when he notices the look of sadness in her eyes. He sighs. "We will help you find your daughter. We will need an item of hers. With your permission, may we take this item back to Atalonia, where the whole pack will begin a search?"

The king looks to a guard and nods. The guard leaves the room. "Tristan, I know of the wars before peace, where you fought the dragons greatly."

Tristan doesn't like where this is going. Damoc approaches him. "Alpha, this will be suicide."

The king speaks again. "The dragons know that this is *not* a war, and they intend to help seek out the princess. No harm will come to either party."

"Damoc," says Tristan, "I trust the king to keep to his word." Damoc steps back, fighting the urge to shift into his wolf form.

The side door opens and a female comes in. Tristan finds her scent familiar. She doesn't look up; she just hands him the garment and dismisses herself quickly through the same door. Gladonis and Itisha watch Liza's retreat with confusion. "Gladonis," says the queen.

He pats her hand. "Yes, my love, I noticed that too."

The two turn back to Tristan and notice he is looking to the door with a confused look on his face. Itisha leans towards Gladonis and whispers. "He recognises Liza."

"Damoc, did that female look familiar to you?" asks Tristan.

Puzzled, he looks to his king. "No, she didn't."

Frowning at this, he dismisses the woman from his mind, yet it still niggles at him. With this, they excuse themselves, telling the king and queen that a search party across the land will commence when they get back, and that word will be sent through Damoc or one of the dragons.

"Tristan, did that servant look familiar to you?" asks Itisha.

"I do not know."

****

On the way back, Tristan feels as if he is running from something, but he cannot place the feeling. With Damoc at his side, he wonders if he detects his hesitation. He almost turns back several times on the way home. It takes them four days.

Once they return, the other packs come to greet them. "We will all meet in the throne room." The packs depart, leaving Tristan and Damoc behind. "Damoc, I fear I have misplaced something, but I don't know what."

Damoc looks at him. "Alpha, we have misplaced nothing. Unless you dropped the garments given to you, all is well." They walk in silence to the throne room, where they give the other packs orders to seek out the princess, not resting till she is found. They also explain that the dragons will be working at their sides.

After this, Tristan returns to his room. Damoc watches with concern but lets him be. Tristan feels at a loss and finds himself restless, so he tries going to bed, but he tosses and turns all night.

****

I take in my surroundings. The dungeon has shackles hanging from the walls. Moss is in the cracks and all over the stonework. Ivy has grown through a crack in the window. I am thankful that it is summer, for I won't freeze to death. Breathing in through my nose, I gag. It smells of stale urine and faeces. Looking to the floor as best I can over my arm, I notice dark marks staining the floor. I hope it isn't blood, but knowing it is. There is also a pot in the corner. I frown, not knowing what it is for. I don't understand why I am here, let alone why someone trusted took me. A single tear escapes my eye. I am thirsty and hungry, and I need the toilet, but I cannot move and I refuse to call for help. There is nothing to do but think. I hope my parents are okay and have sent a search party to find me, but I wonder, with the spell, if they will be able to. *Drakus—does he even know I am missing? What of the war with Tenalp? I pray Father has stopped the threat of war.*

The sound of a key in the door distracts me. Staring straight at the ceiling, I refuse to look at the man who enters. Without a word he approaches the cot and releases me from the bindings. My skin is red and sore, and my body aches to move, but I do.

"Follow me," he says.

I get up, still not looking him in the face. He turns. I notice he is wearing a multi-coloured cloak. Oh, it hurts to move, but through gritted teeth I slowly walk. It is the longest corridor I have ever seen in a dungeon, and I walk up the stairs behind him. The light coming through the window nearly blinds me. I raise an arm to shield my vision until it adjusts to the light. I notice that I am in a kitchen. It looks like it has never been used, as cobwebs are in the corners. There is a slight crack in the window, allowing a breeze, and there is dust at least three inches thick on all of the surfaces.

Looking around in the corner, I notice a small table that holds a bowl, a roll and a jug. My stomach grumbles and I look straight to the floor, noticing that my feet are black and my dress is beyond repair. "Eat," he says. When I don't move, he pushes me forward.

"Do. Not. Touch. Me," I say. The next thing I know, I'm in the air, unable to move. I start panicking and look him straight in the eyes.

He grins. "Foolish girl." My screams vibrate through the castle, and blood flows from my whole body. I don't know what is happening. I can feel myself growing weak with the pain; it's unbearable. My screaming subsides, and my head rolls forward. I see the floor moving towards me, and I fall into the blood I had just lost moments ago. Shivering and weak, I cannot get up. I close my eyes.

I wake up screaming and shoot into a sitting position. My body has deep gashes on it but are no longer bleeding. I curl up into a ball, noticing it is dark outside, with nothing but the moon for light. I cry until sleep claims me.

Zeva and Drakus are in my dreams. They are at the other end of a field. I try running towards them, but no matter how much I run I cannot reach them. I start screaming, but they don't hear me. I wake with a start to find my captor is watching me.

"They will never find you. Follow me."

With a heavy heart, I follow. He knew of my dreams. Of course he did; he was a mage. I'm determined to try to dream of other things or not sleep at all.

Soon we are back at the kitchen. "Eat," he says. Through tears, I eat and drink. "Good, Zaferia. You will need your strength."

I look to him. "Mage, when the people realise you took me, you will be killed. I may eat your food and obey you, but it is only so that I can see you die. You may suspend me in the air and torture me, but you will die, and this satisfies me greatly." With that I rise. "I presume I am to return to the dungeon to be tortured – or would you rather do it here?"

He looks to me, grinning. "You have a lot of hatred, Zaferia; that will do nicely where you are going." He smiles the most evil smile I have ever seen.

"Where is that?"

He walks straight up to my face. "Why, you're going straight to hell."

CHAPTER 10

"How do you intend on doing that? The only hatred I carry is for you, mage. My heart is full of love for many people; that is my passage into heaven. I do not fear you or the torture you put upon me; you are a traitor." I walk past him, enter the corridor, and make my way back to the dungeon, where I sit and wait for him to deliver my punishment.

Nightfall arrives, and he still does not turn up. I lie down and fall asleep.

I shoot up awake and realise it's morning. I look to the door and see it's open. *Is this a trap?* Slowly I walk to the door and peep around the corner. It's dark, but I cannot see anyone. I start walking up the steps and make my way back to the kitchen. At the same table as before, my food is laid out. I walk to it and wolf it down. Hearing a noise I don't recognise, I run straight back to the dungeons. When I go through my door, I freeze on the spot. There is fresh clothing and towels. I look to the left and spy two pots; one is full of warm water. After closing the door, I strip, wash myself all over, and get dressed.

Then I sit and wait for the traitorous mage to come back and torture me. Listening, I hear footsteps nearing. Bracing myself, I stand up and try to control my breathing. I face the door, ready for him. He has a strange-looking stick in his hand and has changed into different robes; they are a pale brown with a gold hem. I look at him with disgust.

"Ah, Zaferia, shall the torture commence?"

I look him straight in the eyes. I try to show no fear and nod. I soon find out that the stick holds magic. It tears through my skin without even touching me, and no blood leaves my body.

Over the following days, my screaming lessens as the torture worsens. Every morning, I wake, go to the kitchen, eat, and look out of the window. There is no courtyard and plenty of land – enough for Zeva and the other dragons to land. There are so many trees. There is no point trying to escape; the door always throws me back, and when I try smashing the windows, objects just bounce off. *Why is there a crack in the dungeon window but it won't budge? Should there even be a window in the dungeon? Why am I thinking of these things?* I let out a frustrated scream and storm back into the kitchen and start cleaning it to control my anger. When I am finished, it is sparkling. Satisfied, I walk around the place.

I finally find the courage to go looking for a mirror. When I see one, I walk to it slowly. I gasp and drop to the floor, screaming. Getting control of my breathing, I start to get up to take a closer look, but I don't recognise myself. There are scars all over my face and neck, one running from my hairline all the way to my collarbone. I think it is from one of the first couple of times he marked me. Looking to my chest I notice a mark. Leaning closer to the mirror I see it is circular with a pentagon within, and in that there is a creature with horns. Frowning, I wonder if I really am going to hell. The mark isn't rough to the touch; it is just raised. *How come I didn't notice it before? The mage didn't do this; the markings are different.*

I turn around and start making my way to the dungeon. There are clean clothes on the bed. Sighing, I change.

"Zaferia."

The sound of his voice makes me jump.

"In seven days you will be dressed in preparation for your fate. The hatred that you have for me has grown stronger every day; the demon will be most pleased." With this he walks out of the room. I sit there not knowing what to think or feel. "Oh and Zaferia, war on Tenalp continues, and no one searches for you. Such a shame your true love could not have been interested enough."

I lie down, and silent tears leave my eyes. I pray he is lying. Drakus had been in my dreams, looking at me as if I were the only woman alive. I know my parents will not rest until I am safely home. He said 'in seven days,' but I am unsure how long I have been here. I start to mentally count down the days. I figure I have been here thirteen days. *Maybe he is right, he could have put a spell on them to forget about me.* I rise from the bed and start walking around the torture chamber. I head for the front room to look upon the world.

All of a sudden, I have pains in my chest that I cannot explain; they send me to the floor. It can't be the mage, as he has left. Struggling, I get to my feet, and the pain becomes a feeling of longing and love. *Could it be?* I struggle to the window, looking for any sign of my love, but I see nothing, so I run around looking through the other windows, noticing there are none at the back. *Odd; there should be windows, not rock.* The feeling goes, and I am left standing, lost. *What was that?*

I stay by the window until it is almost dark, and my stomach rumbles. I make my way to the kitchen to eat. It's strange; there always seems to be food ready at the table, steaming hot. I have no idea where it comes from, but I sit, eat, and drink.

****

Tristan wakes with a start, sweating. Throwing the covers off, he realises who she is, and he is furious. "How did she get there? Who let her out of the dungeon?"

Instead of pacing his room, he goes in search of Damoc. Upon reaching the throne room, he all but growls for him to come out. "Damoc, where are you? I demand your presence at once!"

"Tristan, what is wrong? You have awakened the females and younglings."

Growling, Tristan walks up to Damoc. "Who let her out of the dungeon? Why is she a servant at Caturn?"

Damoc has a confused look on his face. "Tristan, we have not had a human for over two years, le …" His voice breaks off as it dawns on him that the female servant at Caturn was the one who stabbed Tristan. "Surely it is not possible."

Tristan picks up a chair and throws it across the room, growling. He starts to shift.

"Alpha, do **not** do this."

With that Tristan shoots straight past Damoc in wolf form, vowing to kill her. He feels his inner wolf growl. He runs so fast he makes it to Caturn in two days, hardly resting.

CHAPTER 11

He goes to where they had left the clothes from the prior visit and gets dressed as he marches to the courtyard gates, he yells at the guards, "Tell your king that Alpha-King Tristan of Atalonia demands his presence at *once*." A guard runs into the palace. Tristan paces in front of the gate while he waits, just as furious as when he left home.

"The king will see you."

Tristan marches straight to the throne room and opens the doors, growling at the guards. He enters just as Gladonis sits. Once there, he has no idea what to say or how to say it.

"Alpha-King Tristan of Atalonia, did you drag me away from my beautiful wife just to stare at me? Is there word of my daughter?"

He shakes his thoughts free. "No, there is no word of your daughter. I came for a different matter, but it will keep. My apologies." He turns to go, wondering what an earth he had been thinking. "Tristan, why are you here?" The closeness of the voice startles him. Turning around, he realises it is the queen. *Oh, this just gets better.* Bowing, he gives his apologies.

Itisha places a hand on Tristan's arm. "Please sit; you look drained."

He sits at the advisors' table with the queen, and as he looks up he notices the king joining them. Looking to the queen, he notices she too looks drained and there is nothing but darkness under her eyes. "My queen."

"You may call me Itisha, Tristan."

He looks at the queen. "My apologies for demanding your husband's presence. I ... I allowed my anger to take control; forgive me."

Itisha looks at him for a long time; she sees hurt, anger, betrayal, and love in his eyes. "Tristan, please speak freely."

He looks to the king, who nods. "Itisha, I wish I brought word of your daughter." Seeing her eyes glass over, he hesitates. She places her hand on his, urging him to continue. "We lost her scent at the waterfall. I have wolves searching the surrounding lands in pairs, but they have yet to return with news. Her scent was followed to Falor, but we understood you knew of this. We have searched for eleven days now, my queen; her scent has been masked well." At this she squeezes his hand harder. "We will not rest until she is found. I am sorry, but I am here for another reason." Itisha pats his hand, urging him on. "A female servant that you have here – I have come to take her back to Atalonia."

Gladonis stands, paces, and then turns to Tristan. "Who do you speak of, and why do you want her?" Tristan is at a loss as to how to tell them. He decides on the truth. "A few years ago a woman who was not part of the pack stabbed me. No one knows where she came from or who she is. When I came here before, I detected a scent that was familiar. Now I know why; she is the one who stabbed me whilst I slept. She was placed in the dungeons and escaped. It is the servant who brought us the garment. With your permission, I would like to take her back with me." Gladonis looks at him for a while, but the queen does not move.

"The one you speak of is not just a servant; she is my daughter's friend. I will not hand her over knowing she will be killed. Zaferia will come searching for her. You have put me in quite a quandary, my friend." Tristan looks at the king. "Liza was found by my daughter, close to death, her clothing torn to shreds, bleeding heavily from deep gashes all over her body." He looks to Tristan, who is feeling an anger stronger than any he has ever known, with a look all too familiar, through gritted teeth

"I never touched a hair on the woman. I do not intend to; she is human. I will not break a peace treaty." Itisha stands, and Tristan automatically stands as well. "Sit, please, Tristan. There is no need for formalities." He did as requested. "Guard, fetch me Liza; tell her to dress warm."

"My queen, what will Zaferia think? I forbid this."

Itisha walks up to her husband, placing a hand on his face. Tristan looks down at this point. "My love, My king, I remember when we first met. Do you?" Puzzled, Tristan looks up to see Gladonis place his arms

47

around Itisha, linking his fingers behind her lower back. "How could I not? I still bear the scar above my heart, which has beaten for you ever since." Tristan clears his throat.

Itisha takes Gladonis's hand in hers. "Let her go with Tristan, for I saw love in his eyes as he spoke of Liza. He will not harm her, my love"

Gladonis looks at Tristan. "What my wife says – is this true? You feel for a woman who stabbed you?"

Looking at them both, he sighs. "Yes, I do. I cannot explain it."

Gladonis smiles. "You bring me back memories, boy."

There is a knock at the door, and the king tells the visitor to enter.

Liza enters slowly. She freezes on the spot with her eyes fixed on Tristan. "Liza, you have gone deathly pale; come sit." When Liza doesn't move, Itisha walks her to a chair opposite him. Liza never takes her eyes off him; nor does he look away. Her heart is racing. Gladonis and Itisha give each other a knowing look, and then Gladonis clears his throat, breaking the spell. Liza looks down. "Do you know this man?" Gladonis asks.

Looking Tristan straight in the eyes, she says, "He is not a man; he is a wolf."

Gladonis walks to Liza, who looks up at him. "Explain how you know him."

She glances straight back at Tristan, who has a bemused look on his face. "I tried to kill him, my king – unsuccessfully, it seems." Looking back to the king, she hears a low growl. She looks back and sees that he is looking furious; the brown in his eyes showed more clearly when he was mad, a rare trait for a wolf. Feeling calm around him, she smiles and looks back to Gladonis.

Tristan is furious. He wants to kill her then and there until she looks into his eyes. He can then feel himself turning into putty. He is hooked.

"Liza," says Gladonis, "he has come to take you back to Atalonia."

She turns straight to him. "I will go nowhere with this … this wolf."

Tristan is about to speak, but Gladonis beats him to it. "He has given us his word; no harm shall come to you."

She looks at the king. "And you believe him?"

Gladonis is taken aback by this and raises his voice, "Remember your place, Liza; especially if you want to talk to me like that."

Tristan growls straight at the king, and Liza grimaces. "My king, I am sorry. He lives with wolves; I am human. I need to be here when Zaferia gets home; else who will look after her? I will not go with some … some pack of wild animals." Tristan stands and growls so loudly they all face him.

Itisha intervenes. "Desist with the testosterone levels at once, Tristan. What you are asking is difficult, Gladonis; Liza is scared. You both must apologise to her at once."

****

Drakus frowns. "Very well, Marcus; I trust your word. For now I just feel like a fool; I am also angry, for if I had not sent her away, she would be safe with me where she belongs. I miss her. I sit in the garden when I cannot sleep; the smell of the lavender reminds me of her. I close my eyes and I can see her."

Marcus has no idea what to say in response, so he just sits there looking at Drakus, who starts laughing. "Forgive me, Marcus; I seem to be going soft." Marcus just nods, and Drakus gets up. "I go in search of my true love; you may continue with what you were doing." Drakus makes his way to the front door, alerting Zeva he is waiting for her.

When she arrives, they search until the early hours. "Oh, Zaferia, I am so sorry. I beg for your forgiveness. I wish you were here, looking into my eyes, where I see so much love and trust." Zeva lets out an almighty roar, agreeing with Drakus.

CHAPTER 12

Both kings are shocked but do as the queen asks. "There, now can we continue like adults? Liza, you hold your tongue."

Gladonis speaks. "Tristan's pack searches for our daughter, Liza." She looks at him, gives a slight smile, "Thank You" then looks back to her king. "As you are aware, so do the dragons. The moment Zaferia is found, word will get to you after us. If you do not arrive, I will send war to Atalonia in your honour."

She cannot help the gasp or the tears that block her vision. She looks at Tristan, and he simply nods. She is speechless. "What do you plan to do with me, wolf?"

He is amused at her hidden threat, but he is determined not to get fed up with the battle she is giving him. He hopes for her sake as well as his he will not kill her. *Damoc is going to kill me and war will be brought amongst my people.* "I will not harm you, Liza; nor will anybody else."

A bolt of lightning strikes her heart, and she looks away from him for a moment. "You will allow me to return once Zaferia is home?"

Noticing that her tone is now softer, he looks at her, noticing a change. "Liza, you will return back to Atalonia once the princess is recovered. May I ask a question, Liza?"

She nods.

"What happened after you left the dungeon?" He notices her paling and fighting back tears weakly.

"I will not speak of it, wolf."

He is determined to kill whoever caused her so much pain. *She is mine.*

Gladonis then says, "Tristan, how are you getting Liza to Atalonia?"

He looks to Gladonis. "She will ride on my back."

Liza looks startled. "I will do no such thing, my king, if I may borrow a horse and supplies to get me to his land."

Gladonis looks from one to the other, having no idea how to answer. Itisha approaches. "Tristan, with your permission – and of course yours, Liza – could you ask Zeva to take you? Your new king seems reluctant to let you leave his side he will have you in his sight."

At the same time they say, "Very well."

Itisha smiles. "Very well. Liza, call Zeva."

A few moments later, they all hear a mighty roar. Liza grimaces, and they all look to her. "She was looking in Mauro with the other wolves and dragons, but she has an interesting message for you, my king."

Tristan looks up and frowns.

"Not you, wolf – my king. It appears that the pegasus king is furious our princess was taken and not alerted. Zeva says he is willing to assist if you make contact. If the spell placed on Zaferia, it may also be as old as the pegasi. Also, he is immune to any form of spell. He is the king of Tolemaz. Please consider asking for his help." She looks to Tristan. "May I gather some of my possessions?"

Tristan manages a nod his brain not functioning.

When Liza leaves the room, they all look at each other. Itisha speaks first, looking at Gladonis. "Do you think what Zeva says is true, my love?"

He sighs. "I do not know. The pegasi have always kept to themselves. The king comes to the meetings with his mage but never speaks. Tristan what do you know of them?" He looks to him.

"Not much, only that they spend most of the time in human form and, as you said, keep to themselves."

Itisha approaches Tristan. He does not like the look in her eyes. "Alpha-king of Atalonia, hear this, as I shall only say it once. Liza is connected to a dragon, as you just heard. If word reaches us of any harm done by you or anyone else on your land, my king and the dragons will rain down on you and destroy everything you have ever built. If you do not keep your word, war will be upon you. *Are we clear?*"

At this moment they hear another roar. Tristan rises from his chair, and Gladonis moves in front of his wife. "King, queen of Caturn, I give you my word no harm will come to Liza. May I suggest a dragon stay close to my land so if anything does happen to Liza both I and Zeva will know? And rest assured I will kill anyone who harms her, for I am alpha-king, I will protect her. All I ask if the war comes is that you spare the women and children – unless a woman has touched my mate; only then will I want Zeva to rip her heart out. I feel this would be an honour for her."

"It will," says Zeva.

He looks at the queen but she doesn't speak, so he looks around the room before sitting.

"It is I, Zeva, Alpha-King."

He looks to the window, speechless.

Itisha stands with her hands on her hips. "Gladonis, here we have true love; do you second it?" After a few minutes she turns to him, touching his face.

"My Itisha, you are a great queen." He kisses her.

Tristan looks down as this occurs. "Zeva."

"Yes, Alpha-King."

"If anyone touches Liza, allow your dragons to rip their heads off and burn them till there is nothing but ash remaining."

"It will be done." He smiles at this.

****

In her room, Liza writes a letter for Zaferia telling her where she is and that she shall explain when she sees her. Realising that she does not have many possessions, she picks up a cloth bag and puts her clothes in it. She walks into Zaferia's room, takes a solitary piece of quartz, and places the note under her pillow. Walking back to the throne room, she hears a commotion. She runs and sees that Rogue is out of bed and being held back by guards. "You! I will get you for this. What did you do to me? Where is my Fe?"

She runs straight into the throne room without knocking and slams the door shut. Out of breath, She just smiles. *Luckily you cannot hear the commotion in here.*

She looks at Tristan. "Does your garden have lavender, wolf?"

He can't help but chuckle. "Yes, we have lavender."

Relieved she will still have Zaferia's smell close, her breathing finally returns to normal. She looks to her king and queen, who are looking at her in puzzlement. "I am ready to leave now," she says. Itisha gives her a warm embrace, as does the king. "I will miss you both dearly."

She walks out of the room and is relieved to see Rogue is gone. She walks quickly out of the palace to Zeva with tears running down her face. "Are you okay, Liza?"

"No, but thank you for asking Zeva," Liza replies while climbing onto her back. Moments later, they are airborne.

"Liza, how is Tristan getting home?" Zeva asks.

"He will turn into a smelly, foul wolf, Zeva, why?"

Oh, Liza, you're cruel."

This makes Liza smile. "Let us surprise him."

"Shall we go and fetch him?"

Just as Tristan starts stripping off his clothes to shift, he is wrapped in talons and lifted into the air. "Liza thought it might be quicker if I took you both," says Zeva.

He feels the urge to kill her. *I am a wolf; we do not fly.* This doesn't stop him from smiling all the way to Atalonia, though. The feeling of the wind tempts him to shift into wolf form; he finds it is a wonderful feeling. He considers asking Zeva to take him in wolf form one day.

****

For four days now, they have been searching the lands for Zaferia with no luck. Zeva is restless, flying about for hours on end. All the other dragons are following suit, occasionally seeing wolves on the ground. Drakus wonders if they ran through the forest too. "Zeva, shall we continue with the search? Meet me at the gate." Drakus notices a wolf on his land, and Zeva enters a protective stance. "Easy, Zeva; remember the treaty."

The wolf shifts into human form and approaches Drakus "Forgive my trespassing; I found Zaferia's scent going this way. "I'm afraid I will have to alert the king of Caturn."

Drakus looks at the shifter in front of him. "Your name, shifter?"

"I am David from the wolf pack of Atalonia."

Drakus nods. "I am Drakus, king of Falor. The king of Caturn knows of Zaferia's presence here, but I understand you are following protocol." The two men are silent for a while.

"Your dragon – her name?"

Zeva steps forward. "I am Zeva, queen of all dragons, wolf."

He bows his head, shocking Zeva and Drakus. "An honour, Zeva." At this Zeva growls and walks away.

CHAPTER 13

"Drakus, we must make haste searching for our queen." Zeva roars, and the sky fills with dragons of all colours and sizes.

Drakus laughs. "We leave to search for Zaferia. I believe you shocked my dragon, David. I'm impressed."

David nods, looks up, and walks away. Turning back into a wolf, he heads towards Caturn.

"Zeva, can you sense her yet?"

"No my king"

"On to Byrond, Zeva."

Drakus feels part of him is missing. He cannot understand the feelings in his heart. "Zeva, return home. I must speak with Marcus." When they get back, Zeva continues her search for Zaferia. Drakus walks into the castle, calling for Marcus. He heads to the throne room, knowing he will find him there.

Drakus finds Marcus sitting at the advisors' table working on something. When he sees Drakus, he moves the project out of sight. Drakus just frowns. "Marcus, I feel a spell has been cast upon me. I need your help."

Frowning, Marcus asks, "What kind of spell do you speak of, Drakus?"

"I fear a spell has been cast on my heart, as the feelings I have for Zaferia are so strong I do not understand them. I dream of her and have done so for two years, but when she came to me to ask for her father's blessing for her hand, I sent her away."

Marcus sits back. He has never heard Drakus speak so freely. "My king, no spell can be placed upon the heart; it is not possible. I fear what you are feeling is true love and guilt. Do not fret; all will be as it should."

****

Itisha and Gladonis watch as Zeva carries Tristan. "He will not be happy, my king."

Gladonis laughs. "No, my love, he won't." They watch from the palace doors until they cannot see Zeva anymore.

"Gladonis, what Zeva said – do you think Konrad will assist us if he is immune to witchcraft?"

"Glador told me that Drakus would find Zaferia, but it has been thirteen days; my patience is wearing thin. I am growing more concerned as the days pass. The last time we saw her, we were not on good terms."

Itisha looks to him, noticing a look of raw pain on his face. She takes his face in her hands, and he feels like the most wanted man in the world. Looking into her eyes, he sees they are lost in each other's love. They walk to the drawing room. "Gladonis, I am sure our daughter is not thinking of that. She is probably worrying about the impending war with Tenalp; she will make a good queen."

He smiles at this. "I will get Glador to send word to Konrad to aid us in our search, but something about this does not feel right. War against Tenalp will cease today"

Holding her close to him, he notices she still wears the same perfume from when they were courting. It reminds him of their youth. "When Zaferia returns, we shall have a party in her honour."

"Gladonis, with dragons and wolves looking for Zaferia, I feel you should hold a meeting with the mages from across the lands. I know it is not a full moon, but I feel they will come."

He sighed. "My queen, I fear they will look at this as a weakness from our side and declare war. We cannot have chaos reigning down."

She tuts. "Gladonis, there has been no war since the treaty. We have Falor, Atalonia and soon Tolemaz searching; they will be on our side. No one will start a war with a princess missing; they will be with us. It may bring our daughter home sooner. I want her home."

He looks to the floor. "I am thinking like a king again and not a father, I shall call upon Glador and hold the meeting tomorrow."

At this Itisha rises. "Very well, my king. I shall retire for the night and leave you with your thoughts." Kissing the top of his head, she whispers "Goodnight." Walking to her room, she lets tears fall.

Gladonis calls for Glador. "My king, is all well?"

"Inform Tenalp there will be no war. Gather the mages from the lands. We shall meet tomorrow." At this he nods and vanishes. Gladonis stands up and makes his way to the bedroom, where he can hear Itisha crying. He goes in, takes off his clothes and holds her until morning.

At breakfast, Gladonis realises he doesn't like the distance between him and his wife, so he picks up his plate and utensils and sits next to her. She looks at him with a grin. "Very unbecoming for a king."

He grins. "From now on I shall sit here, for you are the wiser one."

Both grinning, they continue with breakfast. "My love," says Itisha, "I shall take a stroll through the gardens today, as it is a wonderful morning."

"I will accompany you if you wish."

There is a knock on the door. Gladonis tells the visitor to enter. "Since when do you knock, Glador?"

Glador walks to Gladonis and bows to Itisha. "You are both eating. I have never disturbed you at these times."

Itisha stands. "I shall go to the gardens. I shall wait for you there, my love. Good morning, Glador."

Gladonis watches Itisha leave the room. The moment the door is shut, he looks at Glador.

"You told me Drakus would be the one to find my daughter. It has now been seventeen days!"

"My king, he searches for her. The mages have arrived. They are waiting in the throne room."

Once seated in the throne room, he looks to the mages. "Thank you for coming at such short notice." He notices Damoc and Marcus are absent "I have called you here as my daughter was taken seventeen days ago. No one can detect her scent, and the wolves are finding it difficult, as well as the dragons." He looks to his left. "Wade, mage to Konrad of Tolemaz, is it true that he is immune to all forms of magic and is prepared to assist?"

Wade looks around and then back to Gladonis. "I feel I speak for us all. In truth we expected this meeting sooner. We will all assist you in the search for your daughter. The dragons and wolves have not worked alongside each other in over three hundred years. Our treaty is important to us all."

Gladonis could not speak; he was overwhelmed. A single tear escaped his eye.

"King Gladonis, we are from inhuman lands; what of the humans?"

Clearing his throat, he looks to Wade. "For a long time, my kind has been protected from your way of life and your existence. I will not cause chaos; this is the way I want it to be."

They all nod in agreement. "Please tell your kings I send my apologies for just requesting yourselves. I shall see them on the next full moon." At this they all nod and vanish – even Glador, which Gladonis frowns at. He stands and makes his way to his queen in the garden.

After spending most of the morning and early part of the afternoon with his wife discussing what the mages said, he excuses himself after dinner and goes to see Rogue.

Upon seeing him, Rogue stands. "What of Zaferia? Is she home?"

Gladonis signals for him to sit. "Are you well, Rogue?"

"Sorry, my king. Yes, I am well. I feel ready to return to your side, and with your permission I wish to search for Fe... Zaferia."

Gladonis looks straight at Rogue, having noticed Rogue used the nickname he gave Zaferia when they were younger. He smiles inwardly at this. "The dragons and wolves have started the search. I have just held a meeting with all of the mages. They are all willing and prepared to search for your Fe, Rogue."

Rogue looks to Gladonis, shocked. "How do you know I call her Fe, my king?"

Gladonis laughs. "Rogue, I have known you since you were a small boy, barely able to walk. You have been at Zaferia's side all of your life. I am not deaf or blind."

Rogue looks at Gladonis. "My apologies. I did not mean to insult you. May I ask a question?"

"Of course, Rogue." He looks straight into Gladonis's eyes and takes a much-needed breath. "Where is the witch Liza?"

CHAPTER 14

Gladonis's mouth dropped. "Witch?"

Rogue looks at him, startled. "You did not know she was a witch?"

Gladonis shakes his head.

"At the waterfall, when Zaferia was taken, her captor slit my stomach and throat. She conjured a spell to heal me through her hands. A strange light surrounded her. She healed my stomach but passed out on my lap trying to heal my throat. That is how the guards found us."

Gladonis just looks at him and sighs. "Liza is in Atalonia."

Rogue stands and walks out. The anger radiating from him keeps Gladonis from following.

Looking up, Gladonis notices Rogue walking back to him. Rogue points in his face when he nears the king. "You gave her to the wolves; they will kill her." Rogue walks back out and heads to the armoury, set on getting Liza back and then searching for Zaferia. He determines he will kill the king of Atalonia if Liza is hurt. He feels he needs to see her, make sure she is okay, thank her – witch or not – and bring her home.

"Rogue, you dare to walk away from me? Speak to me with disrespect?"

Rogue stops dead in his tracks and turns to face the king, who is red in the face. "My king, I must head to Atalonia and then on to search for Zaferia. You should not have let her go."

The king gets right in his face, and Rogue takes a step back.

"The king of Atalonia has made an oath that no harm will be brought upon Liza. You speak to me in that manner again and you will be dead. You are lucky I know it is of your concern for Liza and Zaferia that you speak that way, so I will forgive you this time; but boy, remember your place when addressing me again."

Rogue nods. "With your permission, my king, may I see Liza and then search for Fe?"

Gladonis nods. "Take supplies and the finest horse; I will send word to the king of Atalonia."

Rogue nods and walks away. Gladonis walks to the throne room, trying to calm down on the way there. Once in the room, he sits. "Glador," he says.

After a few minutes, he appears. "Yes, my king."

Gladonis takes in his appearance. *Odd – he is not wearing the royal colours.* "Glador, go to Atalonia and tell him Rogue is on his way to see Liza and to expect him in three days."

Glador looks to Gladonis, nods, and vanishes.

Gladonis stays there for a few minutes, wondering what came over Rogue and why Glador was not wearing the royal colours. *What is going on?* He contemplates questioning Glador but decides against it. *Where does he vanish to?* He gets up and decides he will go and discuss his worries with Itisha.

Finding her in the library reading by the fire, he sits next to her. "Glador is acting strange, my love, and Rogue is showing an anger I have never known," he says. "Liza is a witch, did you know?"

Itisha clears her throat. "I have heard Liza and Zaferia talking of witchcraft and a woman with white hair. Yes, my love, I had a feeling."

He looks to her, frowning. "Why did you not talk to me of this?"

Itisha is silent for a moment. "I did not want you looking at her any differently. Liza is a big part of Zaferia's and our lives. I wanted things as they were."

Gladonis nods. "I am retiring, my love. Would you like to join me? She smiles and puts the book down, and they go to bed together.

****

Upon landing in Atalonia, Zeva places Tristan down gently. Liza gives her a hug as best as she can. "Please let me know of any news of Zaferia."

Zeva looks down to Liza. "You have my word. Call me if you need anything." With that Zeva bows. "I will keep my word; will you?" she says to Tristan, and then she takes off.

Tristan notices the tears running down Liza's face and slowly starts to approach her. "Liza, I am sorry."

She turns to look at him, and he can see the fury in her eyes. "Because of you, wolf, I will no longer feel safe; I will always be watching my back, as I tried to kill the oh-so-perfect king of Atalonia. I wish you were dead; I hate you!"

Tristan is furious at her words. He walks to her, grabs her by the arm, and drags her to the dungeons. His pack watches in fascination, as this is out of Tristan's character. The only person who gets up is Damoc, who follows and gets to them just as Tristan throws her in his cell, only he has a key too. "Tristan, what are you doing?" Damoc asks. Liza lands on her hands and knees, scraping her skin and causing her to bleed. "Tristan, give me that key. How dare you treat a female this way!"

Tristan growls. "Remember your place, Damoc." With this Tristan walks off, shifting into a wolf.

Damoc turns to look at Liza. "Are you okay? Did he hurt you?"

Liza looks to him and slowly starts getting up. "Only my pride, wolf."

He looks at her. "May I suggest that you don't call us 'wolf'; the pack will not take to it kindly. I smell blood; do you need dressings?"

She sits down on the bed. "What is your name, w—"

He grins, noticing she stopped herself just in time. "My name is Damoc. I am second in command."

Liza rises and walks to the gate of the cell, Clearing her throat, she puts her hand through the bars. "Damoc, it is a pleasure to meet you; I am Liza." He looks very familiar to her, yet she is unable to recall where she knows him from.

He takes her hand. "It's a pleasure, Liza. Now I shall fetch you more bedding, a pot of water, and dressings for your hands; then I shall go and find Tristan and knock some sense into our alpha; how does that sound?"

Liza smiles. *Where do I know him from?* She nods and then laughs. "It sounds good, Damoc; however, he is not my alpha, as I would not be in here."

He nods and starts walking away. The moment she sees his back, she knows exactly who he is and feels safe, knowing she will not be harmed.

She walks to the bed, strips off the bedding, and puts it by the bars, smiling while doing so. She also slowly kicks the pot to the bars too; even though nothing is in there, she doesn't want it. Then she moves the bed to a more visible point so she can see when Tristan returns for her, which she knows will be in a few hours. She hears someone clearing his throat behind her. Knowing it is Damoc, she turns around.

He lets out a low whistle of approval, looking at what she did in the cell. "Tristan will not be pleased. I see you take it upon yourself to defy him every step of the way."

Liza nods. "But here I will able to see the oh, so great alpha-king's approach. May I have a broom so I can sweep away the years of dust that has built up? Was I the last one in here?"

Damoc nods and laughs. He turns his head and spots a she-wolf. "Fetch a broom at once." She rushes off.

"Why did she look scared of you, Damoc? Are you scary too?" Liza asks.

At this the she-wolf laughs.

The she-wolf approaches Liza, who puts her hand out. "My name is Liza; what is yours?"

The other woman looks from her hand to her face. "My name is Rose."

Liza pulls her hand back and holds the bars. "Rose, would you mind help dressing my hands, as they are bleeding."

Damoc growls a warning at Rose, and she steps back.

"Please, Rose, I cannot do it on my own; my clothing is ruined, and I have no others. I promise you, Rose, I will not hurt you. I just need assistance from a female I can trust, for I am not used to showing any flesh in a man's presence."

At this Rose slowly approaches the bars. "Your hands, may I see them?"

Liza slowly puts her hands through the bars so as not to startle Rose. She holds them palms up.

Rose frowns. "Your hands will need more than dressing, Liza; the cuts run rather deep. Damoc, what is on the floor here?"

Damoc looks to the floor in the dungeon. "I have no idea, but the broom was a wise move, Liza; I wish we could help you in there."

Liza laughs. "I do believe the great alpha-king planned it this way. Rose, will you help me?"

After looking at her for a few moments, Rose agrees. "I shall fetch what is needed to help you heal quicker, Liza."

As rose walks away, Liza says, "Thank you."

"It will be my pleasure, Liza." she smiles and continues out of the dungeon.

When Liza can no longer hear footsteps, she turns to Damoc. "I know who you are. I shall not speak of it; nor will I tell Tristan it was you that helped me escape that night."

He nods his thanks. "Now that you have everything I said I was going to bring, I suggest you bring a chair close to the bars so Rose can see to you. I shall go in search for our – sorry, my – alpha." He hesitates. "Liza, what is your full name?" He realises she has raised her back straight.

"I trust you, Damoc; I will tell you and no other. Please do not tell your alpha. My name is Princess Eliza Riona Albus, daughter to the fallen king of Volkard. Your kind – or something that resembled wolves – attacked my people, making them flee to Prenom, many dying on the way. They even attacked the children. My father and mother were killed. I believe my home is now no more. I came here once after seeing them die, vowing to kill your king. I hid until he went to bed, and once I heard his snoring, I stabbed him. He threw me off him and stood above me, where he just stared at me. He didn't call his guards until he felt blood running down his body. He looked down at himself and then back to me, and do you know what he did, Damoc? He just smiled. As I was about to charge him again, I was grabbed from behind and placed into a dungeon. They didn't even take my knife from me – why?"

"Liza, I would not let them take your knife. What killed your family was not us but something similar called werewolves. When we sensed blood, we shifted and went to kill them, but they vanished. As we walked around, we buried all the dead. When we found the king and queen, the queen's last words were to take care of you. We searched for you but could not find you. Now we know why, as you were here hiding in our king's room. How did he not detect you scent?"

She blushes at this. "Damoc, he was covered in blood. He stripped off and got into bed, where I just waited behind a drape that covered me well. Luckily he threw the clothes and they hit the bottom of the drape." Hesitantly, she speaks again. "Damoc, I know I am safe with you, as it was you that let me out."

He looks around him, making sure he cannot sense the others. "Yes, I did. I made a promise to your mother. We brought them here and buried them in the royal garden. When Tristan opens the doors, I shall take you to them."

He notices she has tears in her eyes. "It seems I owe him an apology; and thank you for looking after them, Damoc."

He nods. "Right. I must go find him, Liza; I shall see you tomorrow."

****

When Wade arrives back in Tolemaz, Konrad is pacing. "What of king Gladonis do we search with approval for his daughter?"

Wade walks to where he is standing. "My king, he wishes you to seek out the princess. She has been missing for seventeen days; all of the mages have agreed. Where and when shall we begin our search?"

Konrad thinks on this. "We shall start at Byrond and continue to Quanitk tonight. Caution will be needed because of the humans. At sunset we shall search the surrounding lands. Tell our brothers to prepare."

Konrad continues looking out of the window, frowning and wondering why he feels so anxious. His heart is aching and he doesn't know why, he made his way to the gardens. He knows it is to be a long night and day, and tomorrow he will need his strength if he is to search for a princess with his magical senses. He doesn't understand why it is so important, but he feels deep within his soul that he – and only he – must be the one to save her.

The search at night proves unsuccessful, and they return to Tolemaz.

At first light he hears noises outside. Looking out of his window, he notices all of the guards have shifted with their satchels around their necks. He grabs his and walks outside and shifts when he reaches them. "We begin our search for the princess of Caturn. Go with caution; and be safe, my brothers." They all nod and take off into the sky, where their wings almost glow with many colours.

After a few hours they are over Byrond, and they fly into a clearing of the trees, shift into human form, and summon their clothes. They make their way slowly to the forest clearing. Konrad speaks. "Something feels …

off. Take even more caution, guards." They walk to an area with houses, where they notice no one is in the streets. No sellers, just carts. This makes them all frown.

"My king, something is not right," one of them says. "It is too quiet. We have not seen a single human or sensed one."

Konrad nods in agreement, frowning. "Split up. Knock on the doors. If there is no answer, enter; but do not touch or remove anything." They all nod and split up. Konrad goes to the building to his right. He knocks and waits a few minutes, noticing the garden is overgrown. He opens the door, and an awful smell assaults his nostrils. He walks in and notices there are at least several inches of dirt and dust covering the surfaces and floor. He follows the smell and finds it is coming from plates on the dining table that hold mouldy food crawling all over with maggots. Jugs are still full of stale water.

Having seen enough, he leaves, breathing in plenty of fresh air after shutting the door. Looking to his left, he notices his men are in the middle of the town. He starts walking to them. "What did you find?"

Alex, Konrad's protector, speaks. "My king, we found mouldy food with maggots. We fear they have been gone for over a week, but to where we do not know. It seems they just vanished; it is very strange."

Konrad ponders this. *Why would they vanish?* He automatically thinks of Prenom. "Let us head to Prenom in our human form and see what we can find out; then I shall go to the king of Caturn with our findings."

****

Entering Prenom, Konrad notices it is quiet too. They find it is the same there: mouldy food and not a human in sight. "Shall we head to Hedorna, Konrad?" asks Alex.

"Yes, my king, we did. Once we have eaten, we shall turn back into our pegasus form, as our hearing is better."

Konrad nods. The feeling in his mind is uneasy, but the feeling in his heart makes him more anxious. He eats with the others and then walks some distance from camp to think alone. *Two villages abandoned – this has never been heard of. I must tell king Gladonis once we have searched Hedorna.*

65

CHAPTER 15

I wake to a strange noise – one that I have not heard before, like a deep growl that shakes the castle. Sitting up, I hear faint footsteps. He has come to torture me again. I just look to the door, too weak to argue or panic.

"Zaferia, put this on." He throws a dress at me. It is the darkest red I have ever seen. I get up to get dressed and notice he is still at the door. I glare at him.

"Excuse me, Zaferia. Where are my manners?" He turns and walks from the doorway.

I undress and put the dress on, noticing it is very soft as I sliding my arms in. It has criss-cross laces along the top of the arms and material hanging from the hands. The material is see-through and shiny. I can't fasten the back all the way, but the dress almost feels as if it is floating. I walk to the door, face him, and walk straight past him, clenching my hands into fists. *I may wear these clothes, but he will never have my soul.* I can feel my hair move, and I stop in my tracks and bring my hand up to it. Frowning, I clear my throat and carry on walking.

"Excellent. You will please him."

I frown as I look at him. "What day is it, mage?"

He grins. "It is the day you meet your mate." I shudder. "Come, you must eat."

Walking with him to the kitchen, I approach to take a look at the mirror I walk past every day. I come to a full stop. My hair is in swirls on top of my head. I have black on my eyes and red on my lips. I look fit to be a queen. This thought used to excite me, but now it makes me feel sick.

"You look amazing, Zaferia."

I walk past him to the kitchen, where I sit and eat. "When do I meet this so-called mate, mage?"

"You will meet him once the sun has gone down. I will be leaving you shortly, but when I return, I shall take you to him."

"Is he the one who marked me, mage?"

He nods. "Zaferia, he is a very powerful demon, and I am his most loyal servant. I have watched you grow since you were born. You will serve him well; he will be proud."

I think on this for a few minutes. "Why me?"

He looks shocked by my question. "You are strong, Zaferia. You have hidden qualities. He will teach you how to use them."

I frown and then smile. "Then I will kill him. Will you be torturing me today? It would be such a shame to ruin this beautiful dress." I wonder if he hears the sarcasm in my voice.

He laughs. "No Zaferia, no torture today."

I find it difficult to swallow, but I fight back the tears and do so, nodding at him.

I should be relieved there is no torture today. Looking to him, I say, "As it is my last day here, may I go outside?"

He looks at me for a while and then sighs. "Zaferia, I will widen the shield I have put in place. You may have this as your last wish."

I let a breath go. I hadn't realised I was holding it and biting my lip. "Thank you." I hate saying it, but not breathing in fresh air one last time would have saddened me more. I look to him and he vanishes.

I finish eating and drinking, slowly stand, and walk to the front door. Hesitantly I reach for the door, waiting for it to throw me back, but it doesn't. I take a deep breath and turn the handle. It opens, and the smell of the land hits me. I close my eyes and slowly breathe in the smell of the grass, the sweet flowers, and lavender. I smile for the first time in twenty days, maybe with death upon me I appreciate the world more now than ever before. I just wish I could see my waterfall for one last time.

Stepping out, I run my hands across the top of the grass. How I have missed the grass tickling my hands. I make my way to the sweet-smelling flowers and sit in the middle of them. After a while I notice something is missing; then I realise there are no sounds and no breeze. *Where are the birds and insects?* I lie down and stare at the sky. Is there really a shield?

Slowly I get up and walk towards the trees, but I am thrown back and land on my bum. I sigh, wishing I can escape. *I wish I knew magic.* Slowly I get up, wipe myself down, and walk back to the flowers. *Maybe I will collect some lavender and search for a bath in the castle.* I start walking towards the lavender and breathe in the scent; it's such a relaxing smell. I gather a large amount and make my way back to the castle.

I find a room that holds a form of bath and frown, wondering how I will fill it, as the taps won't turn. I try for ages to get them to work. *Stupid taps. I want a bath before I die.* I turn to storm out of the room and hear a noise, so I turn around. The bath is steaming with water. I walk to the bath and put the lavender in, saying a silent thank you, and carefully get out of my dress. Funny, I can reach the top of the back of the dress. I carefully place it over a wall in the bathroom and step into the bath, sighing as it relaxes my aching body. But it's painful; the mark is now the brightest red I have seen. It has been changing over the last few days. I wonder what I will do today. *After my bath I might go back outside and eat my lunch.* I stay in the bath for a few more moments and then get out.

After getting dressed, I walk to the kitchen and see chicken and vegetables. I grab some, walk back to the flowers outside, and eat it.

****

Tristan returns hours later in human form feeling far more relaxed. After dressing, he wants to go to his room, but he finds himself walking towards the dungeons. When he reaches his dungeon, he notices it's clean. Frowning, he sees Liza sleeping on the bed in fresh clothes. He breathes in to catch her scent, and his heart yearns to take her in his arms.

"I can smell you, wolf."

He smiles, and she starts getting up. He walks away from the bars as she walks to them and puts her hands on them, looking at him intently. "Tristan, it seems I owe you an apology." He looks at her with an eyebrow raised. "Damoc explained that it was not your people that killed my family, but you tried to defend their honour. I am so sorry, Tristan."

He walks to the bars and starts to lift his hands to hers. Seeing her pulse racing, he lowers him hands. "Apology accepted."

She smiles at him. "If I am to remain here with you, do you think we can come to another sleeping arrangement?"

He grins. "Yes, Liza, we can." He walks towards the door and opens it, standing back to let her through.

She walks slowly to the door. "Why do I feel like you are going to shut the door on me as I get to it?"

He laughs and steps away from the door. She passes through and walks up to Tristan, taking a deep breath. Tristan freezes on the spot. She is so close he can see the gold speckles in her eyes and feel her breath on his skin. It takes all his strength not to grab her. He pulls his hands into fists.

Slowly she raises a hand to his scar and feels the spark of electricity as she touches him. "I can remove the scar if you wish."

He places a hand over hers. "Please don't, Liza." She looks into his eyes, puzzled by the feelings she has for him. She frowns and removes her hand from his, giving him a slight smile.

"Where shall I be sleeping, Tristan?"

He clears his throat, thankful she didn't ask why he wanted the scar to remain. "Come with me." She walks by his side. Noticing the castle lacks something, but not knowing what, she frowns. He walks to a door and stops. "This is where you shall sleep." He opens the door, and she enters.

Gasping, she turns to look at him. "Is this your room?"

He nods, and she tries walking out. He shuts the door and stands in front of it. "You will sleep in here with me."

Liza starts backing up as he walks towards her. The backs of her legs meet the bed, and she loses her balance. Landing on the bed sitting up, she says, "I will not sleep with you, wolf."

He approaches her, and she backs off as much as she can. As she leans on her elbows, he puts his arms on either side of her and moves his face close to her. "You are, and you will." He notices her breathing is erratic, and the smell sends his mind wild. He kisses her softly. Noticing that she stiffens, he kisses her harder and tries opening her mouth with his tongue. She starts to relax, leaning into the kiss. He notices that she has wrapped her arms around his neck, pulling him closer.

CHAPTER 16

He pulls her up on the bed so her head is on the pillows. He then breaks from the kiss and hears her moan, "Tonight, my love, we sleep." He turns her onto her side, pulls the covers up, and pulls her body to his.

Liza is breathing so fast she tries to control it. She is confused at her reaction; she had never been kissed like that, and it took her breath away. Controlling her breathing, she finally falls asleep in his arms. She had never before felt so safe.

Tristan listens to her breathing and realises she has fallen asleep. He notices that her hair smells of the sweetest of honey. Her body fits to his – a perfect match. He had wanted this moment for years, and now that he has it, he isn't letting her go. She is his. He growls quietly, "Mine."

Liza stirs and whispers, "Alpha."

He replies, "Come here, wife." She snuggles further into him but doesn't wake up completely. He decides he will call a meeting with his pack and let them know what is going on. His queen is finally home. Knowing this, he closes his eyes and falls asleep.

Upon waking up, Liza realises she is on her own. Frowning, she wonders if she will get killed if she goes looking for him. Biting her bottom lip, she opens the door and looks out into the corridor and sees no one. She closes the door and follows the distant voices. Did she dream he said she was his alphena and he her alpha? She determines she will ask him when she finds him.

She hears him before she sees him, and she follows his voice. She enters what looks like a throne room to see people moving furniture. Frowning, she sees Tristan approaching her, smiling at her.

"I hope we didn't wake you?"

She nods. "What is going on, Tristan?" He looks around him. "I am having my throne room back."

She looks at him with an eyebrow raised. "Was it not yours before?"

He laughs. "We have always shared the room; it is about time I had it back." She does not know what to say. "Would you like to see where the gardens are, Liza?" She nods, and he takes her hand, leading the way.

Once seated in the gardens, he dismisses the staff. "I hope you are okay and feel safe here, Liza."

She looks to the lavender. "Tristan, at Caturn you asked me what happened. I think it is time that I told you. I managed to escape here undetected. Making my way through the forests of Towpatha, I came across four men and a woman. They said they would help me, so I decided to rest with them for the night. I felt safe knowing a woman was there. I was wrong. She held me down, and they beat me over and over. They tied me to a tree when morning came, and they hit me until I stopped moving and left. I managed to get free, and I staggered through the rest of the woods, but when I came to Caturn's land, I had nothing to support me, and I collapsed while hearing someone scream. I passed out."

Tristan looks at her, trying his hardest not to shift and sprint to kill them. He realises she is staring at him with almost a nervous gaze. "Liza, I would never have seen you come to harm. Even after you stabbed me, all I could see were your beautiful eyes. I wanted you to be with me. I am sorry for everything that has happened. I put you in the dungeon for your safety; I could never hurt you, Liza. Believe me when I say that, as you are the only one to never cower before me. You are well loved at Caturn, as you are loved here by me. Would you stay with me as my alphena?"

Liza lets out a gasp. "After everything I have said to you, you want me to be your alphena? What is that, by the way?"

He takes her hand in his, nods, and kisses it. "Will you be my queen, Liza?" After looking at him for a few moments, Liza smiles and nods. "Yes, my love, I will be your alphena."

Tristan places a ring on Liza's finger, and she gasps. She had never seen such a ring before. She looks to his face. "It has been in my family for many generations. My mother would be proud to see you as my alphena and her daughter."

Liza throws her arms around Tristan. "I love it, Alpha. I will take good care of the ring, as I will of you too. I love you so much, Alpha."

He holds her tighter. "I love you too, Alphena. Always have and always will. We shall rule Atalonia together. With you by my side, we will always be strong."

Liza places her hand on Tristan's face. "Alpha, when do we get married? Can it be when Zaferia is back? It will not be right not having her at my side. I will be by your side till eternity; where you go, I shall follow and stand next to you as your equal. Come on, we must return to the castle and tell everyone the news."

He smiles at her and kisses her nose.

They walk back to the castle hand in hand, and Tristan notices Damoc walking towards him. "Tristan, you now have a throne room. The dining hall is finished, and breakfast is being prepared. Come, let us eat."

He gives Liza a smile, and she nods. Tristan notices the silent conversation between them and realises Damoc knows of her past. Oddly he doesn't feel angry; only relieved that she trusted him enough. "Damoc, how did Liza escape the dungeon?"

Damoc looks down. "I let her out."

Closing the distance, Tristan approaches Damoc. "You are a very brave man, Damoc; now I know why you are my second in command."

Damoc is relieved. "I am sorry I crossed you, my king."

"Damoc, Liza has agreed to be my alphena. Prepare for a wedding; we shall celebrate as man and wife once Zaferia is home."

Damoc smiles at Liza. "Welcome to the family, Liza."

She hugs him.

****

Konrad rises to silence. Looking around, he notices his men are awake. "My king, we feel we should head to Volkard and see if the humans fled there."

Konrad looks to Chad. "I will go. Make your way to Caturn and wait for me there." They nod and take off for Caturn. Konrad turns and heads for Volkard, hoping the humans are there. This makes him fly faster. He gets a strange feeling, and he is knocked down, breaking trees and hitting the ground hard. *A magical shield.* Frowning, he gets up, brushing off leaves and dirt. Looking to the castle, he feels a strong presence; but what alarms him more is the feeling of pure evil lurking underneath the castle behind the shield. He takes off to Caturn at great speed. Time is running out.

When he lands in Caturn, he shifts into human form and summons his clothes and walks to the palace doors. "Notify King Gladonis; King Konrad of Tolemaz requests his presence at once." Looking around, he frowns. "Where are my men?" One guard goes into the castle; the other replies that they have not arrived. Konrad paces close to the doors. When they open and the guard appears, telling Konrad the king will see him in the throne room, Konrad walks quickly and does not knock. Seeing the king on his throne, he bows on one knee.

"Konrad, please rise."

He rises. "Gladonis, we have searched Hedorna and Prenom to no avail. There are no humans in sight; nor can we sense them. It seems they have vanished. My men were supposed to be here on my arrival, but they have not arrived yet. I went to Volkard and hit a powerful shield with evil lurking there. I fear that is where your daughter is being kept."

CHAPTER 17

Gladonis rises. "Are you sure my daughter is there?"

Konrad nods. "Yes. We will need help to rescue her. I fear a mage is holding her captive, as the shield is as old as I am. I will need assistance whilst I break the spell there."

Gladonis looks to a guard. "Fetch the queen and get word to Drakus."

The guard leaves. Gladonis walks to Konrad. "If what you say is true, we need to get word to Liza, who is in Atalonia. Rogue, my guard, has gone in search of Liza and should be there now. He will want to help." Gladonis paces.

Itisha runs through the door to the throne room in her bedclothes and races to Gladonis. "What is it?"

Konrad takes a few steps back, not knowing how to address the queen in her bedclothes.

"My love," says Gladonis, "Konrad has found our daughter. However, he feels there is a mage involved, as there is a shield in place where she is. We will need help from others to get her safely back." He places his cloak over her shoulders.

She smiles and then looks to Konrad. "What mage do you speak of?"

Konrad looks to her. "I do not know, but he is old and very wise, queen."

A knock at the door disturbs them. "Enter," says Gladonis.

A guard enters, bows to the king and queen, and faces Konrad. "Your men have arrived."

"Bring them here."

The guard nods and leaves. Konrad looks to Gladonis and says his thanks.

A few minutes later, Chad, Alex, and Eric enter, nodding to the king and queen. They go to Konrad. "My apologies for our delay," says Eric. "On the way here, we decided to go to Towpatha and Drapana. We found the humans there. They spoke of noises and the ground shaking from Volkard. They fled, fearing for their safety."

Itisha speaks. "If you believe a mage is involved, how will we spread word for the help we need?"

Konrad turns and faces his men again. "Eric, get our men to travel to the other lands as fast as they can to spread word."

"Konrad." He looks to the queen. "If I may be of assistance – if word gets to King Drakus of Falor, he has a dragon who can connect with Liza at Atalonia. You, Falor, and Atalonia should give the required protection for you to break the spell. Make sure word gets to Liza to return at once. Word will also need to be sent to Drawde."

Konrad nods and faces Alex. "Get word to Abila."

****

"Drakus, a pegasus approaches." On hearing this he runs out of the castle, seeing the pegasus shift to human form and approach him.

"Are you Drakus, king of Falor?"

"That I am. And you are?"

"My apologies. I am Eric, guard to the king of Tolemaz. We have come asking for your help and for your dragon to send word to Liza in Atalonia."

At this Zeva growls.

"What help do you require?" Eric looks to Drakus, unsure of how to answer. "My king has located the princess of Caturn. He requires protection and help while he breaks down the shield holding her. The queen of Caturn requires Zeva to contact Liza to tell her to return at once. Also, no mage is to be told of this meeting."

Zeva looks to them. "It is done, my king. Liza is going in search of Tristan and will return to Caturn; she wants me to get her."

Drakus looks to Zeva and nods. "Before you go, Zeva, take me to Caturn." He turns to look at Eric. "I will fly to Caturn and see you there." He climbs onto Zeva and sets off. Eric shifts and follows.

On the way to Caturn, Drakus is full of hope. He will see his love soon; he will fight until Zaferia is safe in his arms. After landing in Caturn, Drakus goes into the castle and approaches the throne room, where he enters, seeing the king, the queen, and another man at the meeting table deep in conversation. He walks to them and clears his throat. "Ah, Drakus, this is Konrad, king of Tolemaz; he was just telling us of his plans. Come, please sit." Drakus sits. "Do you not think we should wait for the rest to arrive? Save Konrad retelling his plans."

Konrad nods and agrees. "Drakus, I will tell you this; does your mage know that we have found Zaferia's location?"

Drakus frowns. "No, my king, he does not."

Gladonis nods. "Very good. We are suspicious of all the mages and need to keep them in the dark."

Drakus agrees not to tell his mage.

****

Zeva flies off to Atalonia, letting Liza know she is on her way. "Zeva, will you be able to bring Rogue back with us?"

"Yes, Liza, but it will take me longer. Tell him to be ready."

When Zeva lands, Liza runs to her and throws her arms around her. She growls at the different scent Liza has. "Liza, you smell of wolf. I should have expected this, I guess. My apologies for growling; I seem rather protective of you."

Liza just laughs. Rogue approaches slowly. "Zeva, when do we leave?"

Zeva looks to Liza and crouches down. "At once." they both climb on her.

Zeva notices Tristan running towards them, so she waits. He looks to Zeva. "I shall see you soon, Zeva; can you send word as to when we are needed?"

Nodding, she takes off for Caturn.

On arrival Liza and Rogue say their thanks and walk into the palace. They knock on the throne room door and wait to enter.

Once they are in the room, Itisha runs up to Liza and gives her a tight embrace, squeezing all the air from her lungs. "My queen, I can't breathe."

Itisha laughs and lets her go, looking her up and down. She notices the ring but says nothing. "Are you well?"

Liza smiles warmly. "Yes, my queen. I am great. No harm has come to me."

Itisha looks to Rogue. "How was the journey, Rogue?"

He nods. "It was well, my queen."

Itisha wraps her arm around Liza and walks with them both to the meeting table. "Liza, you will act on Tristan's behalf and relay messages back to him."

Liza nods. "Right, we just wait for Abila."

A knock sounds at the door, and in walks the palest and most beautiful woman Liza has ever seen. Once Abila is seated, she looks to the others. "My apologies for my late arrival; my mage is rather … protective." The king waves a hand to dismiss her comment, but it bothers him.

"My daughter has been found in Volkard behind a shield cast by a mage. One of ours has her; that is why no mages are present today. Konrad needs assistance breaking the spell; hence this meeting, as he senses evil lurking there."

Liza gasps. "Volkard is my old home. There is no evil there; it was abandoned years ago."

Gladonis frowns. "What happened, Liza?"

She looks to him. "My family was killed by werewolves. I was the only survivor. My parents rest in Atalonia. It has been deserted ever since. It should be deserted and overgrown."

Drakus looks to Gladonis. "My king, Zeva and her dragons will assist in any way that they can. When do we go to Volkard?"

Gladonis is silent for a few minutes. "In a few hours, the sun will set. We will leave in an hour; is that enough time to prepare?"

Abila looks to Gladonis. "We live in the next land. The castle is built into the mountains. We shall await a signal and approach from the back through the mountain. Do you know how many humans are there, Konrad? We have had no need to suspect Volkard, as all seems well there."

He looks to her. "I felt only the slight presence of one human and evil; the mage must not have been there."

Abila rises "You may not want your mages involved, but I will need mine. Her name is Silvanus; she will help us."

Gladonis nods. "Very well, Abila; we shall get a signal to you when help is needed. And thank you."

CHAPTER 18

"Liza, get word to Tristan and his pack to meet us at Hedorna in an hour," says Gladonis. He turns to Drakus. "Tell Zeva to get the others ready, they will fly above us in case we meet trouble." He then looks at Konrad. "Will your men be ready in an hour? What do you need us to do whilst you break the spell?"

Liza clears her throat. "Konrad, breaking a shield will drain your energy. Allow me to assist you." He starts to argue. "That is my princess and only friend. I *will* assist you."

He looks at her, shocked. "You are human; you will get hurt."

She laughs. "I may be human, but I am a strong in magic and very determined. Would you like to find out … king?" She raises her hand and blue flecks appear.

Gladonis notices the atmosphere building and clears his throat, motioning for Liza to put her hand down. "Enough. Konrad, Liza will assist and then Zeva will fly her to safety. Understood, Liza?"

Looking down, she nods, but having no intention of leaving without Zaferia, she determines to do whatever it takes to bring her friend home.

"Okay, the meeting is over. I will see you in an hour at the forest of Volkard," says Gladonis. At this moment all rise.

Konrad hesitates. "Gladonis, the mage will detect a shift in the atmosphere and come seeking it out. What will we do then?"

He looks to Konrad. "Can you do a spell on a dungeon to keep him in if he means to cause more harm?"

Konrad nods. "I will go and do it now if a guard leads the way." Gladonis nods to a guard, who steps forward. Konrad walks to him, and they go to the dungeons.

"Liza, you cannot sneak away from me," says Gladonis. "You are like a daughter to me. Please come here." She walks up to him, gulping when she is in front of him. He pulls her into a massive bear hug. Shocked, she slowly puts her arms around him, praying that the tears don't fall. He lets her go but holds on to her arms. "Are you well, Liza? You seem ... different."

She smiles up at him. "You have been so good to me, never treated me as a servant – you and my queen. May I call you Mother and Father?" Her voice warbles on this.

Gladonis swallows, as he fears he will start crying. "It would be our honour, daughter."

Itisha walks to them and places her hand on Liza's face. "Daughter."

Liza hugs Itisha with tears in her eyes. "I must return to Tristan; I will meet you at Hedorna, Father." He nods, and Itisha wipes her tears away.

Turning to leave, Liza calls Zeva to get her. She sees Rogue, and she throws her arms around him. "Thank you, Liza. I owe you my life. I shall see you soon. I will stand by your side and fight with you for my Fe."

She thanks him and walks to Zeva. realising Rogue said "Fe." *It must be a nickname he calls her.*

Itisha looks to Gladonis. "Prepare for war, my love. I shall fetch your sword and get Rogue to ready your horse."

He looks into her eyes, lowers his head, and kisses her sweetly. "I shall see you back here, my queen." They both walk off in different directions, determined to get their daughter back.

Gladonis leaves the castle. Hearing a noise past the courtyard, he goes to see what it is. He finds a field full of dragons. He notices Zeva, who lets out a mighty roar, and they all bow to him. The others take off while roaring. It sounds like thunder. "Gladonis, king of Caturn, it will be my pleasure and honour to take you to Hedorna."

He is overcome with emotion. All he can do is nod. He walks to Zeva and touches her, noticing her scales are soft to the touch and almost seem to change colour when the light hits them "You are a beautiful, magnificent creature, Zeva. It will be an honour for you to take me. How do I get on?"

Zeva chuckles and lowers herself. "Place your foot on my leg. Just think of me as a large horse." He climbs on with little difficulty.

When they reach Hedorna, Zeva drops him by the forest's edge. "Gladonis, head through the forest; there you will find the others. Be safe; I shall watch from above."

He watches her fly off then turns and walks towards the others. Konrad, Tristan, Liza, Abila, and all of the people of Elandrial are here. They turn to see him and go to one knee, bowing their heads. "Gladonis, King of Caturn, we go forth in your honour. We will get your daughter back," says Konrad.

"Rise. I thank you. The honour is all mine having you by my side. For my daughter, this moment will be remembered for eternity."

They all walk through the forest. When they reach the end, Konrad turns. "Wait here until the shield is down. Liza, if you would join me." Liza steps forward, letting go of Tristan's hand. He watches them walk to the shield, where they join hands. Tristan lets out a growl but does not move forward, as he notices they extend their free hands towards the shield while speaking a quiet chant. As the chant gets louder, the wind blows around them, sending leaves everywhere. They can feel the energy all around the forest, and it seems to make breathing harder.

After a few minutes, the men start to stagger. Tristan looks forward and sees Konrad and Liza each with an arm around the other. He starts to feel real fear for his Liza. He walks towards her, protecting his face from the flying debris. He hears a mighty roar, and he stops. "Not yet, Tristan; the shield is still up. Do not break their connection."

He looks to them and takes a much-needed breath. "Yes, Zeva, I will wait until you tell me." He slowly walks backwards to the others, gritting his teeth all the way.

When he is with the others, he waits for what feels like an eternity. "Go to her now Tristan," Zeva finally says. He doesn't need to be told twice. He runs to Liza, catching her before she hits the ground. He looks to Konrad and sees him drop to his knees. Tristan grabs his arm. "Konrad!"

He looks to Tristan weakly. "The shield is down, but there is another around the castle. I shall need Liza still."

Tristan growls and looks down to Liza in his arms. She is gazing at him. Her eyes are pure gold with white speckles. *Beautiful.* He looks to her hair, noticing it has white streaks running through it. Touching one, he asks, "Liza, what is this?"

She reaches her hand to his face. "I'm sorry I didn't tell you, Tristan."
He looks to her, puzzled. "Tell me what?"

She rises from his arms and floats upright in the air. "I love you." White
light radiates from her, and the others have to cover their eyes. Before them
she transforms into a nymph.

Tristan sees she is barefoot, wearing a flowing white dress. A green
tribal band runs from her wrist to her throat. Looking to her face, all he
sees are her golden eyes.

She goes to him. "My love?"

He places his hand on her face "Always, Alphena." She looks to
Konrad, who is bowing to her. She walks towards him. "Take my hand;
I will give you all the energy you require. Come, we must get that shield
down." He takes her hand, nodding to Tristan. "Tell the others to come,
but with caution."

Konrad and Liza walk over to the other shield hand in hand. Once
there they come to a stop. With goose bumps all over their bodies, they
turn to the others. "*Run!* Run now!" says Konrad. "Zeva, your dragons –
we need you low, war is about to start. Alert Abila we need her." Liza holds
Konrad's hand tighter, and he feels her fear. "Liza—"

"Not now, Konrad."

They walk forward, noticing manticores and chimeras appearing
around the castle. Looking to each other, they breathe in deeply, gaining
the surrounding energy. "Stay close, my love," Liza says to Tristan. "He
has conjured up manticores and chimeras. She turns and feels Tristan at
her side. She strokes his head. "Let's get Zaferia." The rest of the men form
a line behind them, swords drawn.

CHAPTER 19

My captor has been watching from the castle. Noticing that they have broken down the shield, he summons up manticores and chimeras and goes searching for Zaferia. He finds her banging on the kitchen window. He throws me across the room, and I land, sending everything flying. "You said they would not come, but here they are with an army! You will die today!" He grins at me. "What makes you think they will even reach the castle, Zaferia."

I look at him. "They broke your shield; they are stronger than you." At this I get up off the floor. I want to run out of the castle to Drakus. "There is another shield protecting the castle. By the time they break it, you will be dead." I feel the cuts ripping through my stomach, and I scream, knowing I will be heard this time.

Knowing my true love is here, I feel excited, even with the torture that I am being put through. My torturer will be killed; this makes me happy, and I smile. Looking down, I notice no marks are on the dress. It's hard to see the blood, as it's the same colour; but the dress is damp, so I know I'm bleeding. If I can just hold on, I will soon be in my lover's arms, safe. I close my eyes and imagine being in his arms at the waterfall, listening to the birds chirping and watching the crystals sparkling in the water. I feel pain run along my stomach, and I scream. Opening my eyes, I look straight at him. "You will die today. If I die, your master won't have me and I will be free." A single tear escapes my eye. "I love Drakus; he is my mate."

****

The others all start running towards Konrad and Liza just in time to see a shield being placed behind them, trapping them in. Liza looks up, hoping the dragons are within the shield. Luckily they are. The ground starts to shake, and Liza looks to the others. "Prepare for war. Shifters, shift; protect the humans. Zeva, can you sense Zaferia?"

Zeva comes lower. "Yes, I can sense her. She has been out here."

Liza catches the scent of lavender and smiles. All of a sudden, the mages appear next to their kings, except Glador. They all look to Gladonis, who looks ready to kill someone. "Let us fight and get my daughter." They nod and continue to the castle.

Zeva swoops down and lands in front of Drakus, shooting fire to the left. "Manticores, my king; stay close." Drakus looks and sees something he has never seen before – a creature with a body like a lion's, the head of a human, bat-like wings, and a pointy tail. Looking at this manticore, he notices Zeva's wing go up and sees something bounce off her. "Poisonous spines, my king; they are lethal and will kill you instantly." He nods.

The dragons all swoop down, breathing fire and ice in every direction.

Liza turns around, looking for Gladonis, who is not behind them but in front, running towards a manticore. *Foolish man.* She puts her hand out and uses her powers, grabbing him and throwing him through an opening she made in the shield.

"Sorry, Father; I cannot see you get hurt." She looks to Tristan. "Now my full form has taken over. I can handle the shield behind us; don't make any stupid moves, or you will join Father." He lowers his head and growls, walking to her side. She turns to Konrad. "Where is Glador?"

He looks to her. "Can you break the shield from here?"

She shakes her head. "No, it will take both of us. What of Glador?"

He frowns. "He must be in the castle."

Just then they see fire coming towards them. Liza raises her hands above her head and claps loudly, and the fire reflects off some kind of a protective shield and streaks towards a manticore that lets out an almighty roar and then vanishes into thin air. They look to where the fire came from and notice creatures with the head of a lioness at one end, the head of a goat at the other, and tails of snakes. "Chimeras," Konrad and Liza say at the same time.

Liza looks to Konrad. "How did they breathe out fire?"

He shakes his head. "I have no idea."

"Glador has conjured them," Liza says, turning around. "Mages, conjure up phoenixes and firebirds. Zeva, we need ash on the ground for the phoenixes." Zeva roars and lights up spots for the mages. Wade steps forward and recites a spell, and out rise red phoenixes. Marcus conjures up the firebirds. Looking up, he sees so much colour and power within the shield. "Konrad, we must run to the castle and break down the shield." He nods, and they start running to the castle. All of a sudden Konrad comes to a full stop, causing Liza to fall into him. "Konrad, what are you doing?"

He stands there quietly. "Zaferia – she is in trouble; I can hear her screams."

Liza turns pale. "We must hurry, Konrad; please use the energy within the shields to strengthen yourself." Konrad is full of fear; never before has he felt that.

Running towards the castle, Liza hears a yelp. Turning around, she sees two manticores on Tristan. "Tristan! Konrad, go to the castle; I must help him!" She lets go of his hand and runs to Tristan, shooting white lightning out of her hands. The manticores have Tristan pinned to the ground. They also vanish into thin air. She looks around three more have appeared to her left, along with a new monster that looks as if it has three heads. "Cerberuses." She runs to Tristan, who is limping, and heals him, and she then runs back to Konrad. Suddenly she is lifted into the air by an invisible force. She cannot move and is lifted higher, above all the dragons, and nearly collides with one who hits the shield. She screams as loud as she can. Summoning all the strength she can, she manages to break the invisible grip and falls toward the ground at great speed. She is grabbed by talons around her waist. "Thank you, Zeva." Zeva places Liza on the ground and goes to help the other dragons.

Fire and ice are flying in every direction. The more of the manticores they hit, the more appear. Chimeras are making their way to Liza's people. Frowning, she runs towards the castle. As she nears Konrad, she falls to the ground. A loud growl rumbles forth, and Tristan is running towards her. The pain in her stomach is numbing, and she is struggling for breath. Tristan comes to her side in human form. "Konrad, help her."

Konrad does not hear her, for all he can hear is Zaferia's screams; he is feeling her pain. He shifts and flies towards her, screaming.

Tristan looks to Liza, whose eyes are turning black. "Liza, what is happening? Alphena." She places a hand to his face and smiles, and then her hand drops and her eyes close. Tristan roars loudly. He cannot feel her heart beating any more. "Zeva, Liza is gone; she is not breathing. Help her!" He sees talons approaching Liza, and he loosens his grip. "Yes, my king, I will help her." Taking to the air, she roars loudly.

Marcus appears at Tristan's side. He grabs Tristan and takes him to Gladonis, who is crying on the other side of the shield. Tristan walks to him and collapses onto his knees. They hug one another and cry together. Marcus looks to them and prays that what he is about to do will work. He goes to the other side of the shield in search of Liza.

When Marcus gets to Liza, a dragon is protecting her and roars at him loudly "Move, dragon; she does not have much time. I am on your side. Drakus is my king; you know this." The dragon bows and moves out of the way. He approaches Liza. Lifting up her hand, he feels a faint heartbeat, but it is slow. He places a hand on her stomach and one on her forehead, and he chants a spell until he feels her heartbeat return to normal.

She sits up quickly, gasping for breath, looking to him. "What have you done, mage?"

He looks at her confusedly. "I brought you back."

She stands. "You have no idea what you have just done, you fool." She walks away in search of Tristan, with the magic swirling around inside of her getting more intense by the minute. She turns around. "Where is my mate?" He starts walking towards her, but she backs off.

"He is with King Gladonis in safety. I put him there when I saw you being carried by Zeva." She turns and carries on trying to control the magic within her.

CHAPTER 20

Glador has taken me to the window as the torture continues "See your loved ones die." I cry, taking in the scene before me. I'm not sure how much longer I can last. I can feel myself getting weaker by the minute. My love is fighting a creature I have never seen before. At that moment I see Zeva fly past with a white-haired woman on her back. Remembering the stories Liza entrusted me with, it dawns on me that it's her. "Noooooo! Glador, stop it! You're killing them!" I see a pegasus flying towards, us and the creatures in front of him just vanish. "Glador, please stop!" All this time I have blood dripping down me from the cuts all over my body.

I notice more creatures heading to Drakus. "My love." I cannot help the tears, and I drop my head. I cannot watch any more. But as I look up, I see Drakus go to the ground. He is not moving. I scream and start to struggle against Glador's hold. "Drakus!" Blood mixed with my tears blurs my vision, and I hear Zeva's roar fill the sky. "No!"

I look up to see Zeva swooping down, breathing fire. The manticores disappear, making Zeva crash into the ground. She gets up and walks to Drakus, where she nudges him gently with her nose. Letting out another roar, she picks Drakus up with her foot ever so gently and takes off toward the forest. I notice that Liza is walking into the middle of the fight on the ground with one hand facing the castle. Looking down, I see a pegasus heading straight for us. Looking back to Liza, I see her raise her other arm to the outer shield, where Zeva flies through with Drakus. "Oh, my love. You will die soon, Glador." I am thrown across the room and pinned to the wall. I look up to see daggers coming my way. I smile. I'm hit in the stomach with three of them – one in each arm. I don't even scream. I hear something smash as I fall to the floor, where I let the darkness take me.

****

Konrad cannot explain what he just felt, and he sees the ground getting closer. He lands with a thud. Hearing the roars of the dragons, he sees one swoop down to attack a manticore which vanishes, and she goes down into the grass. He gets himself up and is about to take off again when he sees her carrying a human body. "Drakus." He looks to his people and notices they are all fighting and covered in blood. *I must put an end to this before everyone is killed.* He wonders where Liza is, and then he sees something white walking towards the middle of the fight and realises it's her. "What is she up to?"

He continues on to the castle. When he gets close, he starts a chant and feels magic behind him. Realising Liza is helping him from a distance, he gathers speed. The magic feels different; stronger. He hears Zaferia's screams full of pain in his heart. The shield is broken just as he reaches it. He shifts as he breaks down the doors. He summons his clothes and races through the castle.

Liza can feel the magic within her become unmanageable. She summons up everyone and sends them through the shield, opening a gap at the top for the dragons. "Go now, dragons; I need you to live." They go.

After she replaces the shield around the castle, she releases the magic within her with a scream.

****

Gladonis and Tristan are watching Liza; all they can see is blackness coming out of her. Looking to Tristan, Gladonis sees he has Marcus held up against the shield. "Put him down now."

Tristan growls at Marcus but does as he is told and walks to Gladonis. "What is happening to her? What is that black stuff?"

Marcus clears his throat. "I conjured up magic to heal her. She must not have a pure heart; I didn't detect this. I'm afraid she is using black magic."

They turn to see Liza drop to the ground as all the creatures vanish and the shields come down. Tristan and Gladonis run to her in time to see Cassiel float above her, surrounding her in a white light. They see her lifeless body slowly being lifted, and Cassiel wraps her wings around Liza.

87

"No!" Tristan runs faster but is too late; the two rise up until they can't be seen from the ground any more.

"Tristan, can you sense her?"

Tristan looks to Gladonis, puzzled. "I thought Cassiel only took those that have died. I still sense her." They look up, puzzled and quiet. Marcus smiles, knowing what has happened.

****

Konrad taps into his senses to search out Zaferia. Following them, he turns right and into the kitchen. "Ah, King of Tolemaz, I have been expecting you." Konrad looks around and notices Zaferia lying on the floor in a puddle of blood, barely breathing.

Looking to Glador, Konrad notices he is grinning. "Glador, what have you done? This is an innocent girl."

Glador walks in the opposite direction. "What business is it of yours, pegasus?"

Konrad walks towards him, chanting a spell under his breath. "You think your spell will work on me, foolish boy?" Konrad ignores him and continues chanting. Glador stumbles, grabbing a chair for support. "What are you doing to me? No spell can work on me."

Konrad watches him fall to the floor and stops chanting. "A spell that is older than you and held sacred by the pegasi *can* and *will* work on you. You hurt a human and went against the treaty. You killed her mate. Where you are going, there are no powers for you to use for escape." Konrad waves his arm, and Glador vanishes.

****

Konrad walks up to me. Kneeling, he checks my pulse. It is weak but still there. He turns me onto my back and carefully pulls out the daggers. I scream and open my eyes. "Please, no more, Glador."

Konrad lifts me up to rest on his knee and holds me close. "Glador is gone. My name is Konrad. I've come to take you home, Princess."

I look to him and place my hand on his face, leaving blood all over him. "Thank you, Konrad."

He starts to heal the wounds, which causes me to scream in pain, and I grab at his top, begging him to stop. "It hurts too much. Just let me go; my mate is dead, and I am beyond repair, Konrad." He chants something under his breath, and my whole body feels numb. I relax my death grip on what is left of his top. I feel safe, and my breathing returns to normal. It has been a long time since I have felt this. *Will I recover from this?* I wonder. "What did you do? I cannot feel the pain any more. Am I dying now, Konrad?"

He looks to me with great intensity. "You are not dying, Zaferia. I have numbed your body by using a spell. I cannot bear to see you in so much pain." He holds me tighter. "I am going to pick you up now, Zaferia, and take you home."

I fight back the tears. "You used magic. Can you erase memories, Konrad?"

He sighs. "I am sorry; I cannot. It would be too risky. Now sleep."

All I see is darkness as sleep takes me.

****

Konrad carefully picks Zaferia up. "Zeva, I need your help." Within a few minutes, she lands in front of them; she growls when she sees all the blood. "I have healed her as much as I can risk here, but Zeva, I must get her home." Zeva lowers herself as much as she can. Konrad puts Zaferia carefully on Zeva and climbs on himself. Zeva growls quietly. "Sorry, we cannot risk her falling off; I have put her to sleep."

Zeva gets up and slowly makes her way to Caturn. "Zeva, where is everyone?" Konrad asks.

"The other dragons took them home. Gladonis awaits my queen's arrival. I suggest you wake her."

Konrad looks to Zaferia, feeling very protective. "I am sorry; I cannot. She will need to sleep for a few days while I finish healing her body. She wants me to erase her memory, but I do not know what will be erased." They ride to Caturn in silence.

Just before they land, Zeva says, "Konrad, ask her father if you should erase these memories."

"Where is Liza?"

He swears he can almost hear Zeva sigh. "She was taken by Cassiel."

CHAPTER 21

Upon landing, Konrad and Zeva see Gladonis and Itisha running to them. "Zaferia – is she alive?" Gladonis asks.

Konrad gets off Zeva and gently picks up Zaferia, pulling her into a tight hold so that no one can take her from him. Frowning, he doesn't understand why he is feeling this way. "She is alive but weak. I have placed her in a deep sleep. Take me to her room."

They walk back into the castle and go to Zaferia's room. Konrad lays her on the bed. "Get the maids to change her clothing, something loose, as I will need to see her wounds. I will be back shortly. Gladonis, may I speak with you outside?" Gladonis nods and follows Konrad out. "Zaferia has asked me to erase her memories of what has happened. Zeva suggested I ask you." Gladonis looks at Konrad for a few moments and then nods. "I warn you, erasing people's minds is tricky; I may remove other memories too."

Gladonis sighs. "If it takes away the memories of these past twenty days, we can deal with the other ones she loses."

Itisha joins them as they walk and discuss Zaferia's return. "Gentlemen, shall we return to Zaferia? Her memories will be gone; new ones will be made."

****

Liza wakes up in a white room. Startled at her surroundings, she shoots into a sitting position. Looking around, she frowns. "Fear not, Liza; you are in the healing room."

Liza looks to where she hears the voice coming from but sees no one. "Show yourself." A shimmer starts to appear where she is looking, and within seconds a woman's figure materialises. Liza gasps. "Am I in heaven?" The figure smiles at her. "No, child. At the moment you are where we like to call Aleenia – in between earth and heaven." Liza looks to the figure, wondering if she is imagining the wings. Looking up, she notices the woman is smiling. "No, you are not imagining them. My name is Cassiel; I am the angel of solitude and tears. I rarely interfere with your world, but you, my dear Liza, are someone special."

"What do you mean 'special'?" Liza had never seen someone so beautiful.

"Liza, the gown you wear represents who you are now. You are still human, but you will never age. You have angelic powers. Once you have fully recovered, which won't take long, I shall explain everything that you need to know."

Liza gasps when she sees what she is wearing. She stands. Her gown is white with golden speckles and hung down to her feet. It has golden rope wrapped around her waist and over her shoulders. It is soft to the touch. Her sandals are gold, with ribbons that wrap around to her knees.

She sits back down and looks to Cassiel. "What has happened to Tristan and the others?"

Cassiel goes and sits next to her. "They have all returned home."

Liza stands up. "I feel fine. I must return home to my mate." She starts walking around the white room. "He thinks I am dead, Cassiel; I can feel his pain and confusion."

Cassiel walks towards Liza but stops when Liza starts backing away from her. "Do not fear me, child; you will return soon. There is unfinished business for you there, and I have been granted permission to let you face it."

A tear slides down Liza's face. "Who am I? At the battle I felt evil within me. And how am I here?"

Cassiel places her hand on Liza's arm. "Liza, you are the goddess of Mother Nature. I got you as the last of the black magic was used. I brought you here to recover and to teach you."

Liza frowns at this. "Teach me what, Cassiel?"

"Your powers are great, my child; you need help controlling them, or you could cause great damage. You will remain here for as long as it takes, but you will be returned home. Come, I shall show you where you are."

Cassiel waves her hand in the air, and the room is no longer white. Liza looks around, and all she can see is greenery and mountains. "As you are one with Mother Nature, this is what will be around you while you are here."

Liza smiles. "It is breathtaking; Zaferia would love it here." She frowns at this. Feeling a hand on her shoulder, she looks to see Cassiel. "Zaferia is safe. Konrad, king of Tolemaz, has erased her memory. She is at home."

Liza smiles again. "Cassiel, will I have wings?"

Cassiel laughs quietly. "Yes, Liza, you will; but they will come in time and only when needed. You see, they will sense any danger that we feel we or our loved ones are in."

"Cassiel, what colour are my eyes?"

Smiling, Cassiel looks Liza in the eyes. "They are the same colour as your mate's – brown."

Liza smiles. "How is that possible?"

"Mother Nature, my child, Mother Nature. Come, let us begin."

A door appears and they walk along a green corridor to a wide-open green field, where Liza turns around. "Where did the door go?"

"I don't know, Liza. What were you thinking when we entered here?"

Liza thinks for a moment. "I wanted to see the full view with no building. Are you telling me I made the building vanish?"

"As I said, Liza, you have a powerful gift. A thought can become real; a feeling, reality. This is why I need to help you understand your powers."

"So if I made the building vanish, how will it come back?"

Cassiel walked towards her. "Liza, all you will need to do is think of Aleenia and it will reappear."

Liza thought of Aleenia, and it returned. Her mouth dropped with shock, and she heard Cassiel laugh. "Wow" was all Liza could say.

****

Itisha, Gladonis, and Konrad walked towards Zaferia's room together. "Is what Zeva told me true – that Cassiel took Liza?"

Itisha looks at Gladonis as he lowers his head. "Yes, it is true about Liza. Tristan still feels her, though, so I do not know what has happened."

Konrad does not know what to say. Zaferia's door opens, and they walk in to see Zaferia on the bed with a piece of fabric over her top and her lower half. Konrad looks to the maid and turns his back to Zaferia. "She is exposed too much."

Itisha steps forward, looking her daughter over, which brings tears to her eyes. She looks to the maids, who have their heads bowed. "Konrad, all of her body is cut, even the parts that are covered. Heal her; then we will dress her in her nightclothes. She need not know."

He hesitates on hearing the pain in her voice. "No one will speak of this. You may all leave now – except you, Itisha."

He looks to Gladonis. "Post your best guard outside her door at all times."

Gladonis nods. "Rogue is already standing outside her door; I assure you she will be safe with him." He walks to Zaferia and kisses her forehead. "I will see you soon, daughter." He walks to the door and at the same time tells everyone to leave. "Take care of her, Konrad."

He nods. "I will, with my life."

CHAPTER 22

Once everyone has left, Itisha looks to Konrad. "Will she feel you healing her?"

"Yes, and she will scream. It will be hard for you, but the spell I put on her will keep her asleep." He sees Itisha's shoulders sag.

Itisha nods and sits by the side of Zaferia's bed, stroking her hair. "My daughter, I am sorry for what we are about to do." She nods for Konrad to start.

He sighs and walks to the bed. "This will take a few days, Itisha." He looks to Zaferia. "I'm sorry for you too, Zaferia, but I will do as you asked and erase your memories." He looks to her body, wondering where to start, and he notices the mark on her chest. "Oh no."

Itisha looks to him. "What!"

Konrad does not even know where to start with the mark. "I cannot remove the mark given to her."

Itisha frowns. "What does the mark mean?"

He shakes his head. *No, this cannot be happening.* "I'm sorry, but your daughter wears the mark of a demon."

Itisha looks to the mark. "Will she be safe?"

"If the demon does not come in contact with her and I stay close, then yes, she will be safe. No human will be able to protect her. I'm so sorry."

****

My body feels so relaxed. I can hear voices, but they are muffled. I think one is my mother's, but I am not sure. I try to open my eyes, but they are too heavy, so I give in. I imagine myself at my waterfall. I miss it so much. I cannot wait to go back there and feel the water on my skin. I think of the home I want there. *Maybe Father will build me a home away from home.*

All of a sudden I feel pain in my chest and scream. I feel myself rising off the bed and a strong arm trying to push me back down. The pain spreads down one arm at a time then spreads across my stomach and then down my legs. I am sweating from the pain, but I cannot move; my breathing is erratic and my eyes won't open, and I feel myself starting to panic. Then I feel a strong yet gentle hand on my chest, and a relaxing feeling overcomes me. I feel as though I have been wrapped up in the softest of silks.

****

Konrad has never felt so much pain. It is almost as if he is feeling Zaferia's pain and he does not understand it. He has not left her side for three days, not sleeping, just watching her sleep. He sees the nightmares in her mind and places his hand on hers, offering support and strength. After a while he calls for Itisha. He places his hand over Zaferia's heart and feels her pulse slowing. "I have taken away your nightmares, Zaferia. Sleep easy at night. I won't be far from you."

Itisha enters Zaferia's room. "Zaferia is healed," says Konrad. "She will wake up soon. Her memories of what has happened have been wiped, but I do not know what other memories have gone."

Itisha looks at him with tears in her eyes. "Thank you, Konrad. We are forever in your debt."

Konrad shakes his head. "No, Itisha you are not. It was an honour to heal her." He sees a tear slip down Itisha's face.

She gets up and hugs him. "We will celebrate her return when she has recovered. Please bring your people and meet Zaferia properly."

He nods, not knowing what to say. "I must return to my people, but I promise I will return soon. I need to make sure my men are okay." He walks to Zaferia's side and kisses her forehead, and his lips tingle like he has never known before, making him frown.

"What is it, Konrad?"

He shakes his head. "It is nothing, Itisha. I shall head to the dungeons before I leave; there is someone I want to see."

****

Gladonis makes his way to the dungeon to see Glador, hoping to get some answers. Taking a steady breath, he walks to the cell Glador is in.

"You fear me, King."

Gladonis sees Glador chained to the wall by his hands and feet. "I do not fear you, Glador; it is you who should fear me." There is silence as they stare each other out.

"You cannot kill me, King, for you are a mortal; this room will not hold me forever."

Gladonis goes and sits in the chair. "Why did you take Zaferia?"

Glador smiles at this. "Zaferia has always had a destiny since she was born. She is destined to rule the underworld with Nafuna. He has waited patiently for Zaferia to come of age. She wears his mark; she will never escape him and belongs only to him."

Gladonis is about to speak when he notices a shimmering in the cell next to Glador and he sees a look of panic on Glador's face. "Gladonis, get me out of here *now!*"

Gladonis stands and looks to the figure in the corner, and he pales. "Liza, is it really you?"

She walks towards him. "Father, I have missed you. Is Mother well?"

Gladonis collapses in the chair. "But … how … you …"

She smiles. "All will be revealed soon. Could you leave us? I have something I must do." At this she turns around and faces Glador, and for the first time Glador has fear written all over his face.

"Goodbye, Glador. Daughter. I shall see you shortly." Gladonis walks out of the dungeon, smiling for the first time in days, and does not look back.

Liza is staring at Glador, who seems to be frozen in place. "Excellent. Let us begin, Glador."

He shakes his head. "I saw you fall."

She smiles. "Do you like my new look, Glador? I got it in Aleena. You see, I am now a goddess. They allowed me to come back to right your wrongs, and by that I mean to make you suffer, and I have decided I shall inflict the same pain on you as you did on Zaferia."

He looks to her. "How do you know what I did?"

Liza looks to the floor. "It pained me to watch, but the people allowed me to watch what you did. And Glador" – she goes closer to him so she is in his face – "the destruction I will put you through is worse than what you did to my sister." She smiles. "Are you ready, Glador?"

He hangs his head in defeat. "Yes, Liza, I am ready. But know this: Nafuna shall come for you and Zaferia; he will not rest until he has her."

Liza smiles. "That's the plan, Glador. I will kill him."

****

Glador's screams echo all through the castle. "Enough, Liza, you have made your point." She shakes her head and laughs, playing with blue lightning like it's a flower. "No, Glador, I haven't. You *will* suffer, but for now I believe someone else wants part of this."

He looks at her, confused. "Who?"

"You will see soon enough."

****

Gladonis sees Konrad walking towards the dungeons. "Konrad, Glador has a visitor. Do not interrupt what is happening. Allow her to do her thing."

Confused, Konrad stops in front of Gladonis. "A visitor? Who is this person?"

Gladonis smiles. "It is my daughter Liza."

Konrad's mouth drops open. "But Cassiel took her. I thought we had lost her?"

Gladonis places his hand on Konrad's shoulder. "So did I, Konrad; so did I."

Konrad nods and starts walking towards the dungeons quicker than before. When he gets to Glador's cell, he is pressed to his knees by the power within. "Liza."

Liza turns around and immediately dissipates the power in the room. "Konrad, it's good to see you. Please come."

At this the cell door opens and Konrad can feel a force lifting him up. He looks to Liza, shocked. "What happened, Liza?"

Smiling, Liza takes his hand. "I will show you." Konrad had never known the power of someone doing this and was amazed at what Liza had gone through. Liza lets go of his hand, and Konrad drops to one knee.

"Goddess, it is an honour."

Liza laughs. "Get up, Konrad; we have work to do. See, I told you, Glador. Konrad, if you would be so kind, your magic is old – no offence there; you can inflict pain, and I cannot, or I'm limited."

Konrad approaches Glador and punches him hard in the face, snapping his neck. "Konrad, he is to suffer not die." Casting a spell, Liza gives life back to Glador, who sucks in a breath of air.

Konrad laughs. "Liza, is this is what we are going to do? Kill him and bring him back?"

She looks to Glador. "Oh, we're not killing him ... yet. I have questions I still need answers to."

Glador spits on the floor. "I will answer nothing."

Liza looks to Konrad. "Remove his hand, Konrad." Glador screams as his hand disappears slowly, bit by bit. "Ready to answer my questions? We can keep this up all night, as we need very little sleep. Hmm?"

Glador sighs. "What do you want to know, Liza."

She starts pacing. "Why did you do it, Glador? You have known Zaferia all her life. She looked up to you."

He looks at her. "Nafuna requested it. If I know Konrad as I do, he will have erased her memories so that when he comes to claim her, she won't even know what's happening."

Liza stops pacing. "This was the plan all along, wasn't it?" Glador grins. Konrad goes towards him, but Liza stops him. "When? When does he come for her?"

Glador laughs. "Now where would the fun be in telling you that?"

Konrad hits him again, and Liza does not bring him back.

CHAPTER 23

Gladonis hears an almighty roar and knows Zeva is waiting to see Liza. He reaches Zaferia's door and tells Rogue to get some rest, but he refuses to leave until she is awake. "My daughter will want a hug from you, Rogue, when she awakes." Rogue bows his head, and Gladonis sees tears in his eyes. He enters Zaferia's room and sees Zeva at the window. "Tell Tristan his mate has arrived."

At this Itisha shoots out of her chair and runs to him. "Liza is alive? Where is she? Who is screaming, Gladonis?"

He places his hand on her face. "Liza is with Glador, my love; she is well. She is safe, I assure you." Itisha starts crying, and he holds her in his arms and the room is silent. Upon hearing a moan, they both look to Zaferia's bed as her eyes open. They go to the bed in time to see Zaferia smile, and then her eyes close again. "Gladonis, my love, she will wake up soon."

He nods. "Yes, my love, she will."

****

It's been a week since I woke – a whole seven days of bed rest. Rogue has not moved from my door. Well, only to put me back to bed and to eat with me. I don't understand why I have had to rest. To be honest, I don't remember much of the past few years. I was shocked to learn of my age. Liza looks different with white hair, and she is with a wolf!

No one will tell me anything. We are having a party tonight for me to meet the people who live on the island. I have never seen so much of my parents; it's nice.

"Rogue, what time do I have to get ready?"

"You have to get ready now, Fe."

Sighing, I walk into the bathroom and get changed, looking into the mirror. I examine the mark on my chest. Over the past few days is has become more red. I will need to keep it covered; I don't even know where it came from.

Why won't anyone tell me what it is? It's so frustrating not knowing. Shrugging, I get dressed and walk to the dance room. The guards nod at me and open the doors. "May I present Zaferia, princess of Caturn." I groan and see my parents approach me. "Was that introduction needed?"

They chuckle. My father takes me with him. "Come, Zaferia, I want you to meet a very important man." The important man has his back to us, but what I see of him is breathtaking. His hair hangs down to the middle of his back; it is pure white and straight. He has a muscular body. I hear someone clear his throat, and the man turns around. I feel as though time is standing still as I stare into his purple eyes. I don't understand why my heart is beating so fast. He smiles and puts his hand forward.

"Princess, it is nice to meet you."

I am still staring into his eyes when I feel someone squeezing my arm. Looking over, I realise it is my father. "Huh." He raises his eyebrows.

"Sorry, Father, I was in a world of my own; what did you say?"

He sighs. "Zaferia, this is Konrad, king of Tolemaz."

I look into those purple eyes and frown. "Why are your eyes purple?" Realising I said that out aloud, I feel myself blush. "I apologise; that was rude of me. It is a pleasure to meet you, Konrad." I shook his hand and felt lightning, and we both let go and frowned.

"My eyes have been purple since I was born; so were my mother's. It is my pleasure to meet you too."

Frowning, I step closer to him. and he appears to hold his breath. "You seem familiar, Konrad. Have we met before?" He looks straight into my eyes. "Ah, Zaferia, Liza has arrived."

I turn to see Liza. "If you would excuse me Father, Konrad."

I walk in a daze to Liza, who gives me a big hug. I nod to Tristan. "Zaferia, are you okay?" I look to Liza, who is holding me at arm's distance.

"I don't know, Liza; I just met the king of Tolemaz. He looks so familiar, but I don't know where from. Liza, do you believe in love at first sight? I feel like he is my soulmate."

Liza smiles at me. "He is, Zaferia; he is."

I turn around and meet his eyes. My heart feels funny, and we both smile.

"Come, Zaferia," says Liza. "Let us mingle."

I laugh. "Yes, of course, let's.

Arm in arm, we head into the crowd. "Rogue, if you insists on following me, at least walk by my side and not behind me." He shakes his head. "Stubborn man."

I feel Liza nudge me. "Konrad keeps looking over here. Now don't be rude; why don't you introduce us?"

Laughing, we walk to Konrad. He smiles at me. "Konrad, may I introduce Liza, my sister and queen-to-be of Atalonia." They shake hands, and I feel a pang of jealousy. *Strange.* I shake it off.

"Are you okay, Princess?" I look at Konrad, who is looking at my chest, and I realise I'm scratching my mark again.

Liza speaks up. "Zaferia, I am going to join my alpha. Konrad, it was a pleasure." He never takes his eyes off me, and I feel for some reason I can trust him.

"Konrad, I have a mark on my chest. I don't know what it is or where it came from, but I have noticed over the past couple of days it has changed colours and is irritating me." He places his hand on mine. I look back to him, and he has gone white. "Konrad, what is it? You know, don't you? Tell me. Argh, it's burning."

The next thing I know, I am thrown up onto the wall and I stay there.

"Zaferia!"

I look up to see Konrad running towards me. "Konrad!" The whole room starts shaking and opening up, and I see people being thrown out of the room. I scream.

"Zaferia, Look at me, nowhere else. Please look at me." I look to Konrad, struggling for breath. The next thing I know, I feel slashing all over my body. "Keep looking at me, Zaferia. I'm almost with you."

I look him in the eyes as I feel something wet all over my body. "Konrad, hurry! Some … something is happening. Konrad, look out!"

He is thrown across the room, and I watch him hit the wall and fall to the floor. I look to where he was standing, and the creature from my mark is staring right at me. "No, Konrad, help me! Get up, Konrad; get up!" I scream as the creature gets closer to me, and I look to the floor.

"You wear my mark, Zaferia. No one will help you; you are mine."

At this I close my eyes, and a tear escapes. "Who are you, and what do you want from me?" I hear his laugh and find the courage to look up.

"I am Nafuna, king of the undead. I have come to return you to your rightful place"

I smile. "I won't be going with you, Nafuna." He looks at me, confused. I see Liza and Konrad are almost on him. "Now, Liza!" I feel myself dropping to the floor.

Nafuna is flung across the room, and I land in Konrad's arms. "Well, you took your time." He smiles. "Stay behind me."

I smile. "Yes, whatever you say."

He places me protectively behind him, and Liza smiles at me before standing by Konrad. "Shall we?"

He smiles at her. "Let's." They slowly walk towards him.

I feel fire running through my veins. "Erm, guys." They ignore me. "*Guys.*" They stop, and so does Nafuna. They stare at me, and I see a look of shock in Konrad's and Liza's eyes. They look to each other. "Erm, what's going on, and why are you looking at me like that, and why do I feel like I'm on fire?" They start backing away from me, and I take a step forward.

Konrad puts his hand up, and I stop. "Zaferia, your eyes – they're red."

He looks to Liza, and I see Nafuna walking forward. I point towards him, and something shoots out of my finger, hitting him in the shoulder. He screams in pain. "Zaferia, channel your anger and aim it at him."

I look to Liza. "How did I do that, and how *do* I do that?"

"He hurt Konrad, your family; do you feel that anger?" I nod, not taking my eyes off Nafuna. "Now, with what you are feeling inside of you, try to push it out away from you and us; aim it at him."

I nod. *Okay, I can do this.* "This is not easy."

Konrad walks up to me. "I'm sorry," he says.

I frown. "What for?"

"This." He slaps me across the face.

"What the hell did you do that for?" He backs off back towards Liza. "Have I made you angry? Aim that anger at him now. Scream it out of you if you have to."

Breathing deeply, I scream, and I feel the fire down to my toes. I raise my hands out to Nafuna. The next thing I see is red everywhere, and I collapse with the last of my scream.

****

When I come to, we are outside. I look Liza and Konrad over. "Where is he? Where is Nafuna?"

Konrad hugs me. "Calm down; he is gone."

I look to him. "Gone how? Why is the castle on fire?"

They look to each other. "Your mark – is it still there?" Liza asks.

I search for the mark, but it is gone. "No. What is going on?"

Liza gets up. "Come with me, Zaferia." I take her hand. "I will keep her safe, Konrad."

I frown. "Why, where are we going?"

Liza looks to me. "Your home, Zaferia."

The next thing I know, we are standing somewhere hot. "Welcome to your new home, the land of the undead." I look to her, shocked, and then I remember everything. "What shall we do here, Zaferia?"

I look around. "Burn it."

Liza nods. "As you wish."

I imagine myself back with Konrad, and it happens.

"Zaferia, where is Liza?"

I walk towards Konrad, and he starts walking backwards. I smile. "I remember everything, Konrad: Drakus, the fight – everything." He keeps walking backwards. "Stop moving, Konrad." He does so. When I reach him, I place my hand gently on his face. "Do not lie to me ever again."

He shakes his head. "I won't, Zaferia; I am sorry."

I nod and soften my voice. "Good, because it is not fitting for a king to lie to his queen." He frowns, and before he can speak, I pull his head down and kiss him with all I have in me until I am in his arms. "Let's go home."

To be continued…